Skinny Melon
and Me

Skinny Melon and Me

JEAN URE

Henry Holt and Company
New York

Henry Holt and Company, LLC
Publishers since 1866
115 West 18th Street
New York, New York 10011

Henry Holt is a registered trademark of
Henry Holt and Company, LLC

First published in the United States in 2001
by Henry Holt and Company, LLC.
Originally published in Great Britain in 1996 by Collins,
an imprint of HarperCollins Publishers Ltd.

Library of Congress Cataloging-in-Publication Data
Ure, Jean.
Skinny Melon and me / Jean Ure; with illustrations
by Chris Fisher and Peter Bailey.
p.   cm.
Summary: Cherry keeps a diary about her parents' divorce,
her new stepfather, Roland Butter, who draws rebuses for her,
and the coming stepbrother or stepsister.
[1. Diaries—Fiction.   2. Divorce—Fiction.   3. Stepfathers—Fiction.
4. Babies—Fiction.   5. Rebuses—Fiction]   I. Fisher, Chris, ill.
II. Bailey, Peter, ill.   III. Title
PZ7.U64 Sk 2000   [Fic]—dc21   00-39719

ISBN 0-8050-6359-5
First American Edition—2001
Designed by Dave Caplan
Printed in the United States of America on acid-free paper. ∞
1   3   5   7   9   10   8   6   4   2

Skinny Melon and Me

Monday

Skinny Melon and me have decided that we're going to keep diaries.

Skinny is going to start hers on Saturday, after she buys a special book to do it in. She says it's no use doing it in an ordinary pocket diary with spaces for each day because there will be times when we feel like writing a great deal and other times when we may not want to write anything at all, except perhaps what we had to eat for lunch. I agree with Skinny. But I feel inspired to start immediately and can't wait to buy a special book, so I'm using an old writing notebook with wide lines (I can't stand narrow ones).

I think that when a person is writing a diary, they ought to introduce themselves in case it's unearthed in a hundred years, when nobody would know who has written it. I will say right off that this is the diary of me, Cherry Louise Waterton, age eleven (and two months), and I am writing for posterity, in other words, *the future*.

To begin with, I suppose I must put down some facts, such as, for instance, that I'm of average height and neither fat nor thin but somewhere in between, have short brown hair, with bangs, and a chubby round face (I think I have to be honest).

I know that it's round because I saw these charts in a magazine at the dentist's office, showing all different shapes of faces: heart shaped, egg shaped, diamond shaped, turnip shaped, square shaped, and round.

Mine is definitely round. Unfortunately. Round-faced people tend to have blobby noses, which is what I have.

The school I go to is Ruskin Manor. It's not the school I would have chosen if I had a choice. If I had a choice, I would have chosen a boarding school because I think a boarding school would be fun and also it would take me away from Slimey. Anything that took me away from Slimey would have to be a good thing. I did ask Mum if I could go to a boarding school, but she just said, "Over my dead body." She was really pleased when I got into Ruskin because it's the school she wanted for me. She says all the others are rough.

Ruskin is okay, I suppose, though we have tons of homework, which Mum, needless to say, approves of. On the other hand, I have only been there for three weeks, so there's no telling how I might feel by the end of the term. Anything could happen. Our class teacher, Mr. Sherwood, who at the moment seems quite nice, could, for instance, suddenly grow fangs, or the principal could turn out to be a werewolf.

Mr. Sherwood   Principal

I mean, you just never know. (The principal is called Mrs. Hoad. What kind of name is Hoad? It sounds sinister to me.)

My best friend, Melanie, also goes to Ruskin. Her last name is Skinner, and she is very tall and thin,

Skinny Melon

so I call her Skinny Melon, or Skinbag, or sometimes just Skin. John Lloyd, a boy in our class, said last week that we were the "long and the short of it," but that's only because Skinny Melon is so tall, not because I am short.

Skin's face shape wasn't shown in the magazine description. It's long and thin, the same as the rest of her. Sausage shaped, I suppose you would call it. Like a hot dog.

Me and Skin have been best friends since third grade, and we're going to go on being best friends "through thick and thin and come what may." We've made a pledge and signed it and buried it in a plastic bag under an apple tree in my mother's garden. If we ever decide to stop being best friends, we'll have to dig up the pledge and solemnly burn it. This is what we've agreed on.

This is me standing by her.

I live at 141 Arethusa Road, London W5. W5 is Ealing and it's right at the end of the red and green lines on the Underground.

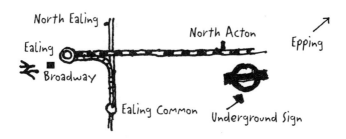

Skin and I once decided to go and see what Epping was like because we had heard there was a forest there, but we got on the wrong train and went to a place called Fairlop instead.

Ealing doesn't have any forests, just a bit of a scrubby downtown that you can walk to from Arethusa Road. There's also a park where Skinny Melon and me take her dog, Lulu, to meet other dogs. I wish more than anything I could have a dog! Well, almost more than anything.

What I would wish for more than anything is to turn the clock back, which is something you cannot do unless you happen to be living in a science-fiction novel where people travel into the past and change things. I would like to travel into the past and change

9

things. That's what I would like more than anything else. But after that, the next thing that I would like is a dog.

Any sort of dog would do. Big dog, small dog, I wouldn't mind.

Big dogs

Small dogs

The reason I am suddenly starting to write this diary is that Mrs. James, who is our English teacher, said that it would be a good thing to do. She said that there are several reasons for keeping a diary. These are some that I can remember:

a. It's good practice when it comes to writing essays for school.
b. It's a record of your life and will be interesting to look back on when you're older.

c. It's a social document (for historical purposes, etc.).

d. It can help to clear out the cupboard.

The class did not immediately understand what Mrs. James meant about clearing out the cupboard, and some people started giggling and pretending to open cupboard doors and take out cans of fruit and stuff and throw them away. But Mrs. James said that the cupboard she was talking about was "the cupboard in your head." She said that sometimes the cupboard in your head gets all clogged up with bits and pieces that may worry you or upset you or make you angry and that writing them down in a diary helps to get rid of them. She said, "We've all got a lot of clutter that needs clearing out." She told us to go home and think about it—to look into our cupboards and see what was there.

Amanda Miles told me the next day that she'd looked into her cupboard, and as far as she could see, it was pretty empty, except for the grudge she still had against Mr. Good, who made her stand in the front hall for throwing water at Andy Innes (which she didn't do). She said that she didn't think that was enough to start writing about in a diary.

"Are you going to?" Amanda asked me.

To which I just made mumbling noises, since there are some things you can't talk about to other people, and certainly not to Amanda Miles. The thing in my cupboard is one of them.

Slimey Roland is the thing in my cupboard.

I'd do anything to get rid of him. I wish he'd go and walk under a bus. I expect Mum would be sad for a while, but she'd get over it. She can't really love him. Nobody could.

I nearly had a heart attack when Mum said she was going to marry him. I mean, I really just couldn't believe it. I thought she had better taste. I told her so, and she slapped me and then burst into tears and said that she was sorry but why did I have to be so selfish and unpleasant all the time?

I'm not selfish and unpleasant. At least, I don't think I am. But it's enough to make you act as though you are, when your mum goes and marries a dweeb. And I had to go to their rotten wedding, which wasn't even a proper wedding, not the actual marrying part. Just Mum and Slime, me and the Skinbag, who came to keep me company, Aunt Jilly, who is Mum's sister, and this man who was doing it. Marrying Mum and Slimey, I mean.

When he'd finished he said that now they could kiss each other, and they did, and I looked at Skin and made this sick face (which I am rather good at), and Skin told me afterward that I was horrible to do such a thing at my mum's wedding. It's all right for her. I know she doesn't have a dad, but who'd want Slimey?

One of the worst things about him is his name—Roland Butter. Can you imagine? I thought at first it was just one of his dorky jokes, like: "Where do pigs leave their cars? At porking meters." Ha-ha-ha—I *don't* think so. Mum, however, said no, that his name is really Roland Butter. He's an artist, sort of. He draws these silly pictures of elves and teddy bears and stuff for children's books, and he has this stationery with a drawing of a roll and butter on it. Mum thinks it's brilliant, but that's because she's in love. If you ask me, it's pathetic, and I am certainly not going to change my last name to Butter, which is what Mum would like me to do. Cherry Butter! How could you get anywhere with a name like that?

Mum's name is Pat, and guess what? He calls her Butter Pat. It's just so embarrassing.

Dad used to call her Patty. She was Patty and he was Greg, unless they were having one of their fights, and then they didn't call each other anything at all except names that I am not going to write in this diary in case it is ever published. It's true that Mum and Dad did have fights often, but what I can't understand is why they couldn't just make up like Skinny and I do.

We had this really awful fight once, me and Skin, about a book I'd lent her, which she lost by leaving it on a bus and then refused to buy me a new one because she said I'd never paid her back the money she'd lent me ages ago when we went swimming and I'd left my wallet behind, which definitely and positively was not true. We had this absolute megafight and swore never to speak to each other again. But life wasn't the same without Skinny, and Skinny said it wasn't the same without me, and so after about a week, we made up, and we've been best friends ever since. Why couldn't Mum and Dad do that?

Dad's living in Southampton now. It's near New Forest and is really nice, but it takes forever to get there. I can't go out with him every weekend like I used to when he and Mum first split up and he was still living in London. Then, he'd come and pick me up and we'd do all sorts of things together—McDonald's, museums, shopping. It was really fun.

After he got a new job, though, and moved to South-ampton, it meant I could only see him on holidays and school vacations.

I could have gone with him if I'd wanted. If I'd *really* wanted. I bet I could. I only stayed with Mum because I thought she'd be lonely. But then she went and met Slimey Roland at some stupid party and got married, and now she's nuts about him, and I'm the one that's lonely, not Mum. So I should have gone with Dad.

Except that Dad's got a new wife named Rose-mary, and he's crazy about her, so maybe he wouldn't want me, either. Maybe nobody wants me. Mum says she does, but how could she go and marry this creep if that was the case? He's really slimy. Look at him!

Ha! He's not the only one that can draw. There's

nothing to it. That's exactly how he looks. Straggly red hair and a beard and this long, droopy face. And he's all freckled with pale skin like a mushroom. Whatever does Mum see in him?

She says that if I love her, I'll try and love Slimey, for

her sake. I've *tried*. But how can you love someone who has freckles and makes these awful jokes all the time? Another thing he likes to do is slip these cards under my bedroom door while I'm asleep. It's sort of creepy. I find them lying there waiting for me when I wake up. They're all covered in sappy drawings, which I think are supposed to be messages. I don't bother to read them. I just throw them straight into the wastebasket.

I know why he's doing it. He's trying to impress me. Well, good luck!

Mum's best friend, Carol, who is my godmother but who has now gone to live in Austin, Texas (though she has promised to send me a real American baseball bat for my Christmas present), told me that Mum and Dad had become unhappy together on account of "developing in different directions," which meant they didn't really have anything in common anymore—apart from me, that is, but I guess children don't count.

Carol said that it's nice for Mum to be with Slimey because they're both in the same business, with Slimey being an illustrator of children's books and Mum being something called a copy editor, which means going through books that other people have written and making sure they've got their facts right and have put all the commas and periods in the right places and haven't called their heroine Anne Smith on one page and Anne Jones on another.

All I can say is that it may be nice for Mum, but it isn't very nice for me. And if writing a diary means clearing Slimey Roland out of the cupboard, then I am ALL FOR IT.

Tuesday

He made another one of his awful jokes this morning. He said, "What's a cannibal's favorite game?" To humor him and keep Mum happy, I said, "What is a cannibal's favorite game?" though, in fact, I already knew the answer because it was a joke that was going around when I was in third grade, for goodness' sake. So he beams into his beard, all jolly ho-ho, and says, "Swallow the Leader!" and Mum groans and rolls her eyes, but in a way that means she thinks it's really quite funny, and I just give this tight little smile and finish my breakfast. It's extremely irritating when grown-ups behave in a childish fashion. Doesn't he realize he's making a complete fool of himself?

I have decided to record occasionally what I eat for lunch, because my school's lunch must be the secret weapon of someone who has it in for children. Skinny asked Mr. Sherwood the other day why he didn't eat in the cafeteria. Skin said, "Is it because you don't want to be poisoned?" Mr. Sherwood said that at his age, being poisoned was a distinct possibility. He said, "My digestive system is no longer geared to the hazards of a school lunch."

If that isn't an admission, what is?

I told Mum what Mr. Sherwood said. I actually put it to her: "If you don't want to lose me, then maybe I ought to take a bag lunch?" All she said was, "Oh, Cherry, don't be silly! What do you want a bag lunch for? You're spoiled, for sure! In my day it was mashed potatoes and soggy green beans and that was that, like it or lump it. Now it's more like a five-star hotel."

I can only conclude that Mum has never been to a five-star hotel. I asked her to name one and she said, "Oh, the Ritz! The Savoy!" I bet the Ritz and the Savoy don't dish up plates of disgusting white worms in congealed blood and call it spaghetti. That's what I had today, white worms in blood. Foul.

Wednesday

Brown worms today. Brown worms in something I won't put a name to because it makes me feel sick. And anyway, I don't know how to spell it. Yeeeeeurgh!

Thursday

There are times when I hate Mum for the way she treats me. Skinny Melon couldn't walk home with me after school today because, guess what? Her mum was taking her to buy a bra! Skinny Melon who is as thin as a piece of thread! Not a bump to be seen. Not even the beginnings of a bump. I am practically a double-D cup compared to her. I mean, she's not even on the chart. But her mum is so nice. She went out and bought Skin's brother a razor for his birthday, even though he hasn't a hair to shave. The Melon hasn't got anything to put in a bra, but still her mum takes her seriously.

She even takes the Blob seriously, for heaven's sake. The Blob is Skin's sister and she's so immature—well, she's only eight years old. She's at the stage of asking these dippy questions like "Where do babies come from?" Skinny's mum never fluffs her off with stories about storks or gooseberry bushes but treats her like an adult and tells her the truth. That's how grown-ups ought to behave. It's hurtful when they laugh at you behind your back, which is what Mum and Slimey do. I'm not saying they do it all the time, but it's what they did tonight.

When I got back from school, Slimey was up in his studio (the back bedroom, which should have been mine). I took the opportunity to suggest to Mum in *strictest confidence* that maybe it was time I, too, started to wear a bra. I said, "If the Melon does and I don't, I'll have an inferiority complex."

Mum said, "Oh, my goodness, we can't have that! But really, why you all must grow up so quickly, I can't imagine."

I said, "Why? Isn't it any fun being a grown-up?" and she replied, "Sometimes it is, sometimes it isn't." So, I asked her, where's the difference? She shouldn't think it's all fun being a kid, because I can assure her it most definitely is not. Not when parents split up and their child is left like an old suitcase. "Who is going to take it? You or me?" And then they both get married again and probably wish there wasn't any kid because, really, she is such a nuisance, always being so selfish and unpleasant. "Why did we ever have her in the first place?"

If Mum thinks that's fun, she must have a very strange sense of humor, that's all I can say.

Anyway, she agreed that we could go to town on Saturday and buy me a bra, so that was good. In fact, I felt sort of warm toward her and thought that in spite of divorcing Dad and marrying the Slime, she was every bit as nice a mum as Skinny's. I thought of what Carol had said about her and Dad growing apart, and I thought that perhaps it was just one of those things that happened and that it wasn't really her fault. I even half made up my mind that in the future, I would try to be nicer to her and forgive her for what she'd done.

And THEN she had to go and blow it all. She went and betrayed me with *him*.

Here's what happened. I'd gone upstairs to wash up, and she was in the back bedroom with Slimey and left the door open a bit. I wasn't eavesdropping, but even if I had been, so what? I think everyone has a right to know what people are saying about them behind their backs. What I heard Mum say was "Hasn't got anything there!" and then go off into these idiotic peals of laughter. I'll never trust her again. I bet old Slimey thought it was *really* funny.

And anyway, I've got more than Skinny has.

Friday

There's a girl at school named Avril Roper whose dog just had puppies. She said if anyone wants one, they can have one free because her mum is only interested in them going to people who will love them. I tore home like the wind and burst into the kitchen and yelled, "Mum, Mum, can we have a puppy? They're for free! And they're small ones, Mum!" I said this because last time I found some puppies, before she married Slimey, they were in a pet shop and cost a lot. They were some breed that was going to grow as tall as the kitchen table and eat us out of house and home. So naturally I thought that since these were free, and were tiny, she'd say yes right away, no problem.

Instead, she just laughed, sort of nervously, and said, "Puppies are always small, to my knowledge."

I said, "Yes, but these are going to stay small. Their mum is a Jack Russell and their dad is a Yorkshire terrier."

You can't get much smaller than a Yorkshire terrier. And anyway, she promised. After Dad left and Mum and me were on our own she said, "We'll get a dog to keep us company." But we never did. Now here I was offering her one for free, so why didn't she jump at it?

Because of Slimey Roland, that's why. I said, "You promised!" and this shifty look came into her eyes, and she didn't want to meet my gaze, which is a sure sign of guilt. She said, "I don't think I actually promised." I yelled, "But you did! You promised!" Mum said, "I may have mentioned it as a possibility. That's all." I shot back, "Well, now it is a possibility! They're going for free!"

And then Mum sighed and said, "Cherry, I'd love a dog as much as you would, but how can we? You know Roly's allergic." I asked, "Allergic to dogs?" How can anyone be allergic to dogs? I know he has hay fever. But hay fever is caused by pollen. Mum answered, "I'm afraid it's not just hay fever. The poor man's allergic to all kinds of things—dust, pollution, house mites. . . ."

And dogs. He just would be, wouldn't he? He's that sort of person. All wimpy and sniffly and red eyed. So Mum has to break her promise just because of him!

Saturday

That creep shoved another note under my door. Something about a turtle. I don't want a rotten turtle! I want a dog. Mum promised.

This morning we went to the mall, and I got a couple of bras, one white and one pink. I suppose they're all right, but it's all gone a little sour now that I know she and Slime have been laughing about it. I keep picturing them lying in bed together having this good laugh.

I threw his note into the wastebasket along with all the others. If he doesn't stop doing it, soon the trash will be overflowing. Mum said today that we're going to have a new regime. She said, "I looked in your bedroom yesterday, and it's a pigsty," to which I instantly replied that as a matter of fact, pigs left to themselves are extremely clean and intelligent animals. It's only farmers that make them dirty by not allowing them to roam free. To which Mum replied, thinking herself very clever, "Well, in the future I'm going to leave you to yourself, and we shall see how clean and intelligent you are. From here on in"—that is a phrase she has picked up from Carol, my godmother, who picked it up in Austin, Texas—"from here on in, I wash my hands of your bedroom. You can take sole responsibility for it. Right?"

I just slumped a shoulder, feeling grouchy on account of Mum breaking her promise about the dog. Mum said again, "Right?" and I muttered, "Right," and Slimey Roland did his best to catch my eye across the table and wink, but I refused to take notice.

Later on, Avril Roper called to find out if we were going to take one of the puppies. I didn't want to say no, so I said we hadn't yet decided, and she said me and Skinny could go and see them sometime if we liked. She said, "They're so *sweet*. You won't be able to resist them. You can hold one in the palm of your hand."

So then I rushed back to Mum and said, "Mum, they're so tiny you can hold one in the palm of your hand! Oh, Mum, can't we have one? Please?" thinking that if I really begged hard enough she wouldn't be able to say no, but she was obviously in a bad mood because all she did was snap at me. She said, "I already told you, the answer is no! Roly's health happens to be of more importance to me than a dog. I'm sorry, but that's that."

I gave her this really venomous look as I slunk out of the room.

Sunday

It's after breakfast, and I'm writing this sitting on my bed. If Mum doesn't clean my bedroom soon, the wastebasket will overflow with notes from Slimey Roland. I'm on strike. Mum *always* used to clean my bedroom.

I used to help Dad clean his car, but Slimey doesn't have one because he can't drive. And Mum no longer has one because of Slimey. He says that cars pollute the environment and we all should walk or ride bicycles. I'm not going to help him clean his bicycle. He looks like a nerd riding about with his helmet on and his goofy little cycling shorts. Like a stick insect with his head stuck in a fishbowl.

Anyway, I help with setting the table and drying the dishes. Mum won't let me wash the dishes anymore because she says I use too much dish detergent. Slimey won't have ordinary detergent in the house; it has to be environmentally safe. He goes around reading all the labels, checking the lists of ingredients, and spying on me and Mum to make sure we don't buy anything that might punch holes in the ozone layer.

Another reason Mum doesn't let me wash the dishes is that she says I break too many things. So now Slimey gets to wash the dishes, and he does it ever so s-l-o-w-l-y and c-a-r-e-f-u-l-l-y, and it nearly drives me mad.

Dad never used to help in the kitchen; it was one of the things that he and Mum had arguments about. But Dad used to be at work all day. Slimey works at home (if it can be called work). It's only fair that he should help.

It wouldn't have been fair if Dad had to help. At least I don't think it would. When I was little and Dad had a good job, we were really really happy. He and Mum hardly ever shouted at each other. It was only when Dad got laid off and couldn't find another job and had to go and start driving a cab that things became horrible. That was when the fights started, because Dad had to do something he didn't like while Mum just went on sitting at home reading her books. Of course she was being paid money to do it, but it wasn't the same as having to go drive a cab. That was what Dad had said.

One thing good about Slimey is that he is interested in Mum's work. Sometimes he reads the books, and they discuss them together. Also, he and Mum don't argue. Yet. They sit and hold hands and do a lot of kissing. I hate to think of them holding hands and kissing all day while I'm at school. It makes me cringe. Kissing someone with a *beard*. I hate beards.

It's eleven o'clock now, and I'm going to go down the road to get the Sunday paper, which is another job I have to do that Mum doesn't take into consideration when she complains about my bedroom. When I come back, I'll call Skinny Melon and see if she's going to take Lulu to the park. Or I might call Avril and find out how the puppies are doing. Imagine having a dog all your own. I could have, if it weren't for Slimey. He's in the back bedroom at the moment, drawing elves, and Mum is downstairs on her word processor, writing to Carol in Austin, Texas. They write to each other every single week. What on earth do they find to say?

141 Arethusa Road

London W5

Sunday 27 September

Dear Carol,

Lovely to have all your news and so glad things are working out for you. Just forget about Martin. He was a jerk and you are rid of him. Some people are better apart. Take Greg and me, for instance. We made each other miserable, yet I couldn't be happier with Roly. I'm sure you'll soon meet someone else, though I confess I live in dread that it will turn out to be some big handsome Texan and that you'll settle down for good in the States! It's a long way to come and visit . . .

You asked how Cherry is doing at her new school. Quite well, as far as I can make out, though she doesn't say very much. Her biggest complaint seems to be the food! She is becoming terribly picky, but I suppose it's her age. I seem to remember when I was eleven and wanted to eat nothing but Mars bars. Ah, those were the days! One Mars bar, one Kit Kat, one Snickers bar, all gobbled up before the morning break and not a spare inch of flesh to be seen! Of course I wouldn't let Cherry eat stuff like that. Roly, fortunately, is educating me in the ways of healthy living. No more junk food. No more snacks. In fact I think we will all end up as vegetarians.

I wish I could say that Cherry's attitude toward Roland had changed for the better, but she is still very cold. It's so disappointing, especially because he tries so hard. He keeps sending her these charming notes with coded messages in the form of pictures. Any other child would be delighted. But Cherry simply throws them in her wastebasket. It's ungracious of her. As a result, I am refusing to clean up her bedroom. She can jolly well do it herself!

Cherry is a bit annoyed at the moment because a girl at school has offered to give her a puppy and she has convinced herself that I actually promised her one. I'm sure I only said that I would think about it. Anyway, as it happens, it's just not possible because Roly is seriously allergic. He's going to start digging a pond in the backyard so that we can have some fish. I think she'll like that.

Oh, I must tell you! It was so funny the other day. Cherry, as you may remember, has this friend Melanie who looks like a beanpole, and Melanie, my dear, was going out to buy a bra! So naturally Cherry decided that she wanted one, too, and we had to schlep out yesterday morning to get her a few. But the joke is that Cherry has nothing on top yet. As flat as the proverbial pancake! Nonetheless, it probably makes her feel sophisticated. Roly says we shouldn't laugh because it's natural to be very sensitive about these things when you are young.

Roly is an extraordinarily understanding person. And sympathetic! Far more than I am when Cherry starts acting up. She has really been trying my patience lately. But Roly never loses his temper. He never allows himself to be goaded. That's why it makes me so angry to watch the way Cherry treats him. He could be such a wonderful dad to her! If only she would let him. I am hoping that the fishpond will do the trick . . .

Write soon! All love,

Patsy

Monday

Dad called last night. He said his new job is keeping him really busy. He's having to work on weekends, and that's why he can't come up to London to see me. But maybe I can go and stay with him in October. He's going to speak to Mum. She'd better say yes! It's the least she can do now that she's gone and broken her promise to let me have a dog.

Old Slimey is digging up the backyard. He's trying to get me interested in goldfish and turtles. He better not think that will make up for not getting one of Avril's puppies. How can you communicate with a fish?

34

Tuesday

Slime stew for lunch today. It had a cardboard lid, which I thought they had forgotten to remove before heating, but John Lloyd said it was a pastry top. All I can say is that it didn't taste like it.

I told Skin about Slimey and his stupid goldfish, and she said that as a matter of fact you can communicate with goldfish, "sort of." She said that they get used to you and will come to the surface for food. I said, "Do they speak to you? Do they play games? Can you take them for walks?" Skinny told me not to be stupid. She said, "A fish is not a dog." I said, "I know that, thank you very much." She then informed me that I was just being nasty "because the fish were Roly's idea and nothing that he thinks of is ever right for you."

What does she know about it?

On the way home from school, we had a disagreement. Well, a bit of a quarrel really. The Skinbag revealed to me that she thinks wearing a bra makes it look as if she has a real bust. Ho-ho! What a laugh! I told her she was kidding herself, and she got snappy and said, "Well, you wouldn't win any prizes! Two goose pimples is all you've got."

I thought that was uncalled for. I mean, you don't expect it from your best friend. We grouched at each other all the way home. Skinny said I was a midget, which isn't true because there are at least two people in our class that are shorter than me, and I said she didn't have any waist, which is true, and she can't deny it. She hasn't any shape at all. Then she said I had a nose like a squashed tomato, and I said she had a face like a hot dog, and by the time we got to her street, we weren't talking anymore, just stomping along in a simmering silence.

I went on simmering all through dinner, because I think it's good to let people stew in their own juice for a while; otherwise they think you're weak. I didn't see why I should be the one to call, when she was just as much to blame as I was. In fact, she was the one who started it, going on about the goldfish. If she hadn't mentioned the goldfish, I wouldn't have said that comment about her bust. It really maddened me that she said I was being horrible to Slime. She ought to try living with him.

For instance, all the time I'm simmering, he's sitting there at the table cracking his fingers, which is this nervous habit he has. Crack, crack, crack, going off like pistol shots. And then he starts making more of his stupid jokes like "What do you get if you cross a witch with an ice cube? A cold spell," until I couldn't stand it anymore, so I went and tried calling the Skinbag. Only Skin's number was busy, but then seconds later, she called me and said she'd tried to get me before but *my* number was busy, and I said, "That was me trying to get you," and she said, "Oh, right," and there was this awkward pause, and then we both spoke together in a rush.

I said, "I'm really sorry I said that about your face looking like a hot dog," and Skinny replied, "I apologize for saying you were a midget." And then we were friends again and started talking about our math homework.

Why couldn't Mum and Dad be like that?

Wednesday

Pond scum and glop pie, and a dollop of cold vomit. Well, that's what it looked like. Skinny and me have this theory about school lunches. We believe they take all the gook that's scraped off the plates and just recycle it. Then they dish it back up and give it fancy names like Cheese and Onion Tart or Lentil Bake. No wonder the staff doesn't eat with us. Mrs. James says it's to avoid the rabble (meaning us). She says, "We like a bit of peace and quiet."

I bet! They like real food and not regurgitated yuck.

Thursday

Rat potpie. Slimey Roland wouldn't have touched it! He's a nutty vegetarian. He said to me yesterday, "You wouldn't eat a puppy, would you? So why eat a lamb?" He has some nerve, talking about puppies. I'm going to see Avril's puppies tomorrow.

Friday

I saw them. They are adorable! They look like little balls of fluff.

Avril's puppies

All of them have been spoken for except one. I came rushing home to tell Mum and she said, "Oh, Cherry, don't start that again," in a pleading sort of voice, which shows she's got a guilty conscience. I said, "But Mum, they're so adorable!" and at that point Slimey Roland came barging into the conversation. He said, "Oh, Cherry Pie, I'm so sorry! It's all my fault. Don't be upset with your mum!"

I hope he isn't going to start calling me Cherry Pie. It makes me want to heave.

Saturday

This is what Slime said to me at breakfast this morning: "By the way, little lambs are rather adorable too."

What has that got to do with anything? I'm not asking for a lamb!

Dearest Carol,

Just a quick note before I have to go and help Roly with the pond. It's coming along! Cherry still refuses to have anything to do with it, but she'll come around. When we actually get the fish, she won't be able to resist it. She's still resentful of the fact that she can't have a dog, and I must say that I would like one myself, and so would Roly. He is not opposed to dogs; in fact, he loves them, as he loves all small creatures (including cranky eleven-year-olds!), but we simply can't run the risk of aggravating his allergy. I think left to himself, he might weaken, but I'm not having him ruin his health just to keep Cherry happy. I know it was upsetting for her when Greg and I separated; on the other hand she is extremely lucky to have a stepdad as warm and funny and caring as Roly.

He'll win her over in the end. I know he will!

Lots of love,

Patsy

P.S. I'm ashamed to say that I still haven't gotten around to telling Cherry about you-know-what. I'm terrified of breaking it to her in case she reacts badly. So far, I've managed to keep it hidden by wearing baggy T-shirts, but it's reached the point where not even the baggiest of T-shirts will hide the bulge! Fortunately, at the moment, she is so wrapped up in her own world that she probably wouldn't notice anyway. But I can't afford to leave it very much longer. As Roly says, it's not fair to her.

Monday

Janetta Barnes found a slug in her salad today. She's taken it home to show her mum. I'm hoping her mum will sue the school and then maybe we'll get to have better lunches.

Tuesday

We all had to line up in the hall after lunch while Mrs. James and Miss Burgess walked up and down looking at us. They said they were looking for interesting faces for the Christmas play. I've been picked to be an angel! A *singing* angel.

I rushed home to tell Mum, thinking she'd be pleased, and all she did was laugh and say, "You? An angel?" I said, "Miss Burgess says I have an angelic face." Mum said, "Yes, you do! I'll grant you that. Isn't it strange how looks can be so deceiving?" I told her that it was a play and that I was going to be acting. I said, "And singing as well, as a matter of fact." Mum said, *"Singing?"* That really impressed her, I could tell. Mum never knew that I could sing. But I can!

Wednesday

All the puppies are gone! Oh, and they were so beeeeeeauuuutiful! I hope they've been taken by people who will be kind to them and look after them. If I had a dog and it had puppies, I would never give any of them away, ever, because you can't trust what people might do with them. There are some people that are just so cruel. Avril says that the puppies have all gone to good homes where they will be loved, but nobody could love them as much as I could have.

Curried compost heap for lunch today. I found

what looked like the remains of a beetle in mine. Janetta says she showed the slug that she found to her mum and her mum said it wasn't a slug but a bit of eggplant, but Janetta is still convinced it was a slug. She thinks it got squashed in her bag on the way home, on account of all the homework we have to lug, and it flattened out. I think her mum just didn't want to admit it *was* a slug.

I've noticed that whenever you tell parents anything bad about school, like rotten school lunches or one of the teachers punishing you for doing something when it wasn't you, parents always take the teacher's side and say, "Well, you must have done *something*," or, "You must be exaggerating." They hate to admit you could ever be right and a teacher might be wrong. I'm dead sure it was a beetle I found, but it's no use taking it home because Mum would only say it was a mustard seed or something.

I forgot to write that Skinny was not picked to be anything in the Christmas play. I suppose her long, thin face is perhaps not as interesting as a round, blobby one, but fortunately she doesn't mind because she has no wish to be an actress. She says even if they had picked her she wouldn't have wanted to be in the play. It's a relief that she's not jealous. On the whole Skinny is a good sport. She has promised to come to one of the performances and cheer me on.

Thursday

Today I ate a plate of cold vomit with dubious-looking objects floating inside. I had this vision of one of the cooks throwing up in the kitchen and someone running at her with a pan, yelling, "Don't waste anything, don't waste anything! Recycle!" Skinny Melon says I'm disgusting, but I just happen to have a vivid sort of imagination.

Skinny came back with me for tea after school, and it was so embarrassing, I didn't know what to do. Slimey Roland was there, all covered in mud from digging the pond in the yard. He looked a sight! I could have died when he came and sat down with us at the table. I was so ashamed of him. And then he started making these awful jokes, the way he does, like "What do you call two spiders who've just gotten married? Newly Webs!" and "What's full of sandwiches and hides in a bell tower? The Lunch Pack of Notre Dame!" I mean, they're just not funny.

Skinny kept groaning and giggling and pretending she was amused. I could tell she was only doing it out of pity for me. It was nice of her, but then Slime started to think he was some big comedy star, and he went on and on till I nearly screamed. Skinny actually choked at one point, and I thought she was going to suffocate, she went completely red. I expect the reason she choked was the fact that he was being so *ex-cru-ci-at-ing*.

I apologized to her afterward. I said, "He's really grungy, isn't he?" I thought we could have a hate-Slimey session but Skinny wouldn't play. She has this thing about fathers, because hers went and died when she was little, and as a result, she thinks even a dad like Slime is better than no dad at all. I told her:

a. He wasn't my dad. (I already had a dad, thank you very much. Just because he isn't living with us doesn't make him not my dad anymore.)
b. She'd change her mind quickly enough if Slimey Roland married *her* mum and went to live in *her* house.

I said, "Imagine listening to those corny jokes every day!" Skinny said that she would be happy listening to his jokes. She agreed that they were corny but said she thought that Slime was "an ace joke-teller." I said, "Oh, do you?" and she said, yes, she did, so I said, "Well, I don't. He's a wimp and a weed and he sniffles." Skinny replied, "So what?" She then had the nerve to tell me that I wasn't being fair.

Friday

The Skinbag must be crazy. She said to me this morning that she thinks Slimey Roland is "really nice." She also said, "Is your mum going to have a baby?" I said, "No, of course she isn't! What makes you think that?" and she said, "'Cause she looks as if she is." So I said, "Oh?" raising both my eyebrows up into my bangs to show I was annoyed. "What exactly is that supposed to mean?" She said, "Well, she's kind of bulgy around the middle."

I told her not to say anything like that about my mum again, so then she said, "Sorry, I'm sure," meaning she wasn't sorry at all, and went into a huff and shut up. We haven't talked for the rest of the day.

How dare she say Mum's bulgy around the middle? That would be like me saying her mum had buck teeth, which she has.

Skinny's Mum's buck teeth

But I would never say that because it would be rude. And anyway, what would Mum want a baby for when she's already got me?

Saturday

I've been thinking about what Skinny said. I have a horrible feeling that it might be true. Mum *is* looking bulgy. I suddenly saw it when she was getting off the bus. And this morning after we'd done all the shopping and were going to have what Slimey calls "coffee and cakies" (he spends so much time drawing pictures of elves that his mind has gone bonkers), I couldn't help noticing that they spent ages standing outside a baby shop googling over all the strollers and cribs and high chairs. They didn't realize I was watching them. They thought I was too busy giving money to a person that was collecting for antivivisection, and I *was* giving them money (because I think that anyone who experiments on animals ought to be experimented on themselves), but at the same time I was watching Mum and Slimey. They had their arms around each other's waists! Mum is going to be thirty-six next year, and I know for a fact that Slime is even older. I don't think people that old ought to be in public with their arms around each other; it looks creepy. Especially when one of them is your mother.

I don't think I could bear it if Mum was going to have a baby. But naturally she would have told me? Maybe she's just suffering from middle-age weight gain.

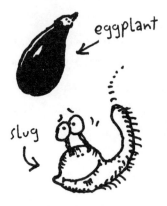

eggplant

slug

While we were shopping, I looked at some eggplants, and they don't look anything like slugs—more like big purple eggs—so I really don't know what Janetta's mum was talking about.

After lunch Aunt Jilly and Uncle Ivo came over and brought their new baby with them. What a horrible creature; it's stinky and does nothing but cry.

Mum and Slimey both drooled over it. Slime kept giving it his bony finger to hold and he made these silly baby noises. I personally think you ought to talk to babies

↑ baby

sensibly, in regular language, so that they can learn things. I don't see any point in filling their heads with

all this goopy sap. I mean, they can't grow up thinking that stuff like "Doo-doo-doo" is how people
communicate, for goodness' sake. They left me alone
with the baby for a few minutes, and I went up to it
and said, "Good afternoon. How are you today?"
and it actually looked at me quite intelligently. I
don't expect it knew what I was saying, but I bet the
words have gone into its head, and I bet they'll be
some of the first words it ever speaks. I bet they'll get
a surprise one day when it sits up in its crib and says
good afternoon to them.

"Good afternoon. How are you today?"

They won't know it's me they'll have to thank.

I'm getting more and more worried about Mum.
She and Aunt Jilly went into the kitchen together to
look at a plant that keeps shriveling, and they were
there for a while, so I went after them to find out
what they were doing, and as soon as she saw me,
Mum gave Aunt Jilly this warning glance, and they
both stopped talking. But not before I'd heard them.
Well, Mum was saying, "I'm really going to have to
work up the courage and tell her."

It doesn't sound good.

141 Arethusa Road
London W5
9 October

Dear Carol,

Many thanks for your lovely long letter! I'm afraid this is going to be another short one, since we've been out walking all day on Hampstead Heath and I am bushed. Getting too old and fat!

The answer to your question, which I know you're going to ask, is no . . . I haven't yet broken the news to Cherry. Yes, yes, I accept that I'm a total coward, but I am going to do it tomorrow afternoon when she gets home from school. Roly has to go away for the night—he is doing a school talk in the north of England—and so it will be a good opportunity. Just Cherry and I on our own. I think she might take it better that way.

We all really enjoyed ourselves today. It was a family outing, the sort of thing we ought to do more often. We took our food with us and had a good old-fashioned picnic! It was Roly's idea, and he prepared all the goodies. He was really imaginative—and it was all vegetarian. Vegetable samosas, sausage rolls made with veggie dogs, vegetable kebabs, soy desserts. I am being won over, and I think Cherry is, too. At any rate, she gobbled everything up. I don't believe she even realized that the sausage rolls weren't made with real sausages! Altogether, it was a super day. It gives me hope that Cherry is coming around at last. I'm just keeping my fingers crossed that hearing about you-know-what doesn't set her back.

Jilly and Ivo came over yesterday with little Sammy, and at first Cherry was very aloof and refused to even look at him. But then we left them alone together for a few minutes, just to see what would happen, and she couldn't resist! Roly reports that she was chattering away nineteen to the dozen. So I think that when she gets used to the idea, she'll be fine.

Cherry has been asked to take the part of an angel in the school nativity play, if you can believe it. An angel! Cherry! She is also going to sing. I don't know if you have ever heard your goddaughter sing? It's not an experience I would recommend! She has a voice rather like a hyena. I only hope they don't discover their error and give the part to someone else because she is terribly excited and looking forward to it. I wouldn't want her little bubble to be burst.

Her friend Melanie came to tea the other day. She is a nice girl; steady and reliable. Cherry occasionally tries bossing her around, but fortunately Melanie can hold her own. I think that's why the friendship has lasted. Melanie won't stand for any nonsense. Roly was there and kept everyone in stitches, clowning around and generally playing the fool. He is instinctively marvelous with kids. I think Cherry was proud of him. She certainly ought to have been.

There! This letter hasn't turned out so short after all. Next time I will report how she takes the news about Mum's big secret . . .

All my love,

Patsy

Sunday

Today we all trailed halfway across London to go for a picnic on Hampstead Heath. On account of Slimey Roland refusing to pollute the environment, we had to go by tube. That meant taking the Central line to Tottenham Court Road, which is thirteen stops, and then hanging around forever waiting for a northern line to Hampstead. We must have looked ridiculous. Slimey was wearing a T-shirt and shorts (shorts! with his legs!) and Mum was wearing a horrible outfit, which made her look frumpy. Definitely middle-age spread. In addition to wearing the shorts, Slime was sporting an enormous backpack. You'd have thought he was going on an around-the-world hike. I wore jeans and was the only one who looked halfway normal.

them

← me

It was a tedious sort of day because all we did was walk on the heath and occasionally sit down and eat stuff and then get up again and do more walking and then sit down again to have a drink. Then they wanted to read their Sunday papers, which was actually fine because it meant I could go off on my own, which I did, and I met this girl throwing sticks for her dog. She let me join in. Hers was a really good dog, a German shepherd.

Anyway, after all that we got on the tube and came home again. What was supposed to be the point of the trip? If they wanted to go for a walk and sit on the grass and eat lunch, then why not just go up the road to the Common? Why trail all the way to Hampstead Heath? Mum says it's because Slimey used to live there before he married Mum and moved in with us and made my life a misery. Well, she didn't say the last part.

Dad was supposed to call me this evening, but he must have gotten tied up. Mum said I can go stay with him during October break. A whole week! Hooray!

The food today was pretty unbearable, for a true carnivore such as myself. Vegetarian sausages, for heaven's sake! I just munched in silence, not saying anything. I could tell that Mum was really enjoying herself, and I didn't want to spoil things for her. But if she thinks I'm going to become a nutty vegetarian, she is kidding herself.

I'm really looking forward to tomorrow because HE is going to be away. He's going to go and bore some poor little kids at a school in Newcastle, showing them his pictures of elves. That means Mum and I will be on our own! Double hooray!

Monday

It's just as well I made up with Skinny Melon today because it turns out she was 100 percent right. My worst fears have come true. Mum is going to have a baby.

She broke the news to me after dinner, just as I was thinking we could have a cozy evening all to ourselves like we used to before Slimey came. She said, "I know I should have told you months ago—" and then she didn't get any further because I said, "Months? You mean it's been going on for months?" and she admitted that it had. She said that she is going to have it "sometime in the new year . . . on or about Valentine's Day." That's February 14! No wonder she looks so big.

I hate Slimey Roland worse than ever now. Doing this to my mum! I bet it was his idea. He's all gooey about babies. Mum would never have thought of it herself. She and Dad were going to have another one once, only she decided against it, so if she decided against it with Dad, why would she go for it with Slime? She certainly can't want to have a baby that's going to be all red and freckled and look like a fungus?

She kept trying to butter me up. Trying to make me feel better about it. She kept saying things like

"It'll make us a stronger family" and "It'll be nice for you to have a brother or sister." I don't want a brother or sister! I hate babies! They mess themselves and cry all the time. And its last name will be Butter and it'll belong to them, to Mum and him, and I'll be an outsider.

I'll never forgive him for this. Never!

Tuesday

I told Skinny Melon this morning that she was right, and she said, "Oh, you're so lucky! I wish my mum would get married again so that we could have another baby."

There are times when I think that Skinny is not quite right in the head.

After school we had a rehearsal for the Christmas play, and those of us that are angels were taught the angels' song. We each get to sing one verse on our own and then the chorus all together. Mr. Freely came in while we were doing it and said, "My good-ness, Cherry has some voice!" One or two of the others put their hands to their ears and complained that I was deafening them, but you have to sing loudly if people at the back are going to be able to hear you, and it is a rock nativity, after all. Not the wishy-washy churchy kind. That's why Miss Burgess chose me, because I have this grand voice.

I really enjoy singing. It's made me wonder whether I ought to try to be a rock star when I'm older. I know it's an overcrowded profession and that last year I thought I might want to be a judge, but being a rock star would bring joy to a lot of people's lives whereas judges often do the exact opposite.

This is me being a rock star.

Oooh!!

This is me being a judge.

Maybe I could be a judge after I've finished being a rock star, since I don't think you can be a judge until you're old. By that time, I would most likely be bored with the other. I once heard someone say that fame could become very wearisome.

Actually, the reason I would like to be a judge is so that I could say to children when their parents are trying to get divorced, "Do you want them to get divorced?" and if the children said no, then the parents wouldn't be able to do it.

I'd have said no. I didn't like Mum and Dad fighting, but I hate living with Slimey Roland and that Dad has another wife. What I'd have said is you've got to turn the house into apartments, one upstairs and one downstairs, and Mum can live in one, and Dad can live in the other, and I could live in both of them and go upstairs or downstairs as I liked. That, I think, would be perfect.

Or else they could have sold the house and bought two smaller ones next door to each other and knocked a hole through the middle. They could live in Southampton so that Dad could still work at his new job. They could have cottages with chimneys and little yards.

And Dad could go off to work, and Mum could stay at home and read her books, and they wouldn't have to see each other if they didn't want. They could even go out with other people, I wouldn't mind, just so long as they came home at night and were always there.

I said all this to Skinny once, and she said that if she had a dad, she'd want him to live in the same house with her and her mother and her brother and sister and for them all to be together. This would be her idea of heaven.

I agree it would be mine if Dad could come back and he and Mum didn't fight.

There's a boy at school named Timothy Dunbar who lives with his mum during the week and his dad on weekends. He says it's great because his dad spoils him rotten, giving him presents and taking him to cool places, which he never did when he was at home. But it's all right for Timothy Dunbar. His dad only lives a few streets away, and his mum hasn't gotten married again.

Slimey came back tonight. Worse luck. I was hoping he might have fallen through a crack in the sidewalk.

Wednesday

Mouse droppings and jellied eyeballs. Or maybe it was frog's eyes. Either way it was disgusting.

Now that Mum has told me about the baby she seems to think it's okay for her to keep on talking about it. She said to me at teatime, while Slime was upstairs with his elves, "What do you think we should call the baby? Think of some names!" I said, "There aren't many names that go with Butter." I said, "Barbara Butter, Brenda Butter, Belinda Butter," very sarcastically, but that was the wrong thing to do because Mum immediately thought it meant that I was interested. She said, "Would you like it to be a girl?" Very quickly, and just as sarcastically, I said, "Bertram Butter, Bruce Butter, Bernard Butter." All Mum said was "Bernard's nice! I like Bernard."

Bernard Butter? She has to be joking!

Slimey Roland brought me back a china figure from Newcastle. It's a Victorian lady with a crinoline, and the crinoline is made of real lace.

my Victorian lady →

Mum says it's valuable and that I must be careful not to break it. It's nice, I suppose. I put it on the top shelf near my bed.

I would much rather have had a dog.

Thursday

I found something new to worry about. Suppose Mum dies while she is having this baby? People do die. In olden times they were always dying in child-birth. Even today it could still happen. I couldn't sleep last night thinking about it.

Friday

I asked Mum two things when I got in from school and to both of them she said no.

First of all I asked her again if I could take a bag lunch instead of having school lunch because today the meal was something unspeakable; I mean, it looked as if it had been scraped up off the pavement. It's only a question of time before I get poisoned. Mum said, "You can take a sandwich so long as you're prepared for it to be vegetarian," which as far as I'm concerned is the same as saying no because I am not going to change my eating habits just to please Slime. What's being a vegetarian ever done for him? Made him look like a fungus. And anyway, it would mean he'd won.

So we had a bit of a dispute about it, with me saying why couldn't I have ham or bologna and Mum saying because it upsets Slime to see dead things in the fridge (and me thinking but not saying that it upsets me to see Slime in the house) and that it's my choice to eat meat at school but we're not going to have it at home. Except I shall probably be dead of food poisoning soon enough, so I suppose it really doesn't matter.

Anyhow, after we finished tea, I said, "Oh, by the way, Gemma Parker has invited me to her sleepover tomorrow. Is that okay?" and Mum tightened her lips and said, "Well, no, as a matter of fact, I'm afraid I don't think it is. I think I'd prefer that you stay away from Gemma Parker."

I knew she'd say that. She got it into her head that Gemma is a bad influence because last year she heard her say a four-letter word that she doesn't even know the meaning of. Gemma, that is. It was just something she'd heard her brother say. All the boys say it; all the older ones. Even Skinny's brother, who Mum thinks is such a "nice young man." They go around shouting it at each other. It doesn't mean anything. They think it makes them sound grown-up.

I said to Mum, "Everybody else is going. I'll feel left out." She said, "Not everybody can be. There wouldn't be room for them." "Well, everyone who is anyone," I said. "The Melon, for instance. Her mum doesn't mind."

Mum likes the Melon. I thought it would sway her, but it didn't. After ten minutes of arguing, she said, "Look, I'm sorry, Cherry, but it's final. I don't want you going to the sleepover." I shrieked, "Why not? When the Melon is allowed to?" Mum said, "You don't have to shout at me. What Melanie's mother allows her to do is neither here nor there. She probably doesn't know that family as I do. I just don't trust them."

The only reason she says this is because Gemma's mum smokes cigarettes, and Mum and Slimey think that anyone who smokes cigarettes is some kind of criminal and ought to be locked up, and also because Gemma's dad happens to work in a place called Franco's that once was raided by the police, which is hardly Gemma's dad's fault. He can't help where he works. What Mum doesn't understand is that Gemma is innocent. She's like a six-year-old. Her mum won't even let her watch television without supervision in case she sees something she shouldn't.

I tried explaining this to Mum, but she didn't believe me. She said, "If you ask me, Gemma's mother is rather flighty."

What does she mean, flighty? Does she think she's a witch or something?

Mum told me not to sulk. She said that to make up for not letting me go to Gemma's sleepover, we'd all go for pizza tomorrow night and then to the video shop so that I could choose whatever video I wanted. That cheered me up a bit. I thought I'd get something really scary that they normally wouldn't let me watch. Honestly, what does she think we do at sleepovers? We don't do anything! We just sit and talk and try on each other's clothes and then tell scary stories in the dark. Gemma's such a baby, she usually falls asleep.

I'm going to get a horror movie, something gross even.

Saturday

I'm seriously annoyed. They wouldn't let me have any of the videos I wanted. Mum said I was just picking them to be a pill. She said if I couldn't choose something sensible, then she would have to choose it for me. When I pointed out that she had promised me, she said, "Oh, now, Cherry, act your age! You know perfectly well there are limits."

She never said anything about limits. She said I could choose whatever I wanted.

"Anything sensible," she said.

They cheat all the time, grown-ups do.

So while I'm moping about looking for something sensible, and doing my best to find one they'd loathe, she and Slimey are wandering over to the kids' section. Suddenly I hear Slimey cry, "Oh, look, Butter Pat!" (I nearly died. The girl behind the counter had to put her hand over her mouth to stop from laughing.) "Look, Butter Pat! Look at this . . . *Snow White and the Seven Dwarfs!*"

And Mum squeaks, "Ohh! *Snow White!*" in a silly little girly voice, and claps her hands. "I haven't seen that since I was younger than Cherry!"

Slimey says, "Me neither. It used to be my favorite film when I was five years old." And Mum says,

"Oh, we've got to have it! Cherry, it's all right, we've found one . . . we're going to watch *Snow White!*"

Which we did, whether I liked it or not. And for the most part I did *not*. I mean, it's kids' stuff. Mum and Slimey sat on the sofa together going oooh and aaah and "Oh, I remember this part!" "That part always terrified me!" It was a nostalgia frenzy.

Afterward I called Gemma and spoke to Skinny. I asked her how the sleepover was going, and she said they were watching *When Harry Met Sally,* which I have already seen, though I wouldn't have minded seeing it again. At least it would have been better than *Snow Sappy White.* I said, "I'm surprised Gemma's mum lets her watch that," remembering certain parts. Gemma's mum is really strict, in spite of being "flighty." Skinny said, "She's sitting there with her finger on the fast-forward button in case of dirty parts, but she can't always get there in time!" We both giggled.

When I went back in the den, Mum said, "It's good to hear you sounding so cheerful." I just frowned. That's the second time Mum has broken her promise.

71

Sunday

Dad called this morning. He said he and Rosemary are really looking forward to having me visit soon although it's unfortunate that I won't be able to stay with them for the whole week, since they are both working and can't get more than a few days off. He said they're very disappointed about this, but they are not freelancers like Mum and Slimey. They can't just take time off whenever they feel like it.

I said that I understood and that it would be great to get away, if only for a few days. Dad said, "Why? Are you frustrated? You're sounding a bit fed up." So I told him about Mum breaking her promises, not letting me have a dog or choose my own video, and Dad said, "Breaking a promise is one of the worst things anyone can do." Of course, I agreed with him.

He said, "I can't offer you a dog, but when you come to visit, you can watch whatever video you like, and that is a PROMISE." I said, "You mean it? Any video I like?" and he said, "Any video except *Snow White* and those silly dwarves." And I hadn't even told him that was what Mum and Slimey made me watch! He said that they kept pushing it on him at his local video shop, trying to make him rent it.

"Don't," I said. "It's really lame."

Dad said, "I won't, don't worry! I was taken to see it as a kid and had nightmares for months afterward."

Nightmares? What on earth could he have had nightmares about? Dad must have been an extremely timid boy.

When I told Mum about Dad and Rosemary not being able to get time off, she gave this sort of sneer, with her lip hooped up.

73

"It's because they both have real jobs," I said. "They can't just go taking days off whenever they want, like you can."

"Of course they can't," said Mum in a snide voice.

"Well, they can't," I said. "They have very important jobs."

"I don't call being a computer programmer all that important," Mum said. "Nor being an office manager," she added.

It's Rosemary who's the office manager, Dad who's the computer programmer. They both work in the same office, which is probably nice for them.

I said, "If their jobs weren't important, nobody would care if they took time off," and to my surprise old Slimey jumped in and agreed with me. He said, "She's absolutely right!" and I saw him give Mum this funny little frown. I don't know what he did that for, but anyhow it stopped her from trying to tell me that Dad isn't important, which I really resent.

Slime said, "The way I see it, everyone is important in his own way." To which Mum snapped, "Her!" being a bit of a feminist, which I am as well. So then old Slime says, "His or her. I stand corrected," and goes on to say that he doesn't see why a person that sweeps the road, for instance, should be considered any less important than a prime minister. But I think that's stupid. Anyone could sweep the road. Not anyone could be prime minister. And not anyone could be a computer programmer, either, so there.

My dear Carol,

Well, I've done it! My secret is out. On the whole she has taken it very well; far better than I'd thought. To begin with, I could see she was stunned—as she had every right to be—and a bit put off that I hadn't told her sooner, but I apologized and admitted that I was a coward, and I think she understood.

I was dreading that she would feel resentful and that we'd be in for a sulking attack, but the other day she was suggesting names to me and even started to sound enthusiastic. I realize now that I was wrong to keep it from her—Roly said all along that I was—but I'm hoping no real harm has been done. I'm making sure that we spend some time every day talking about the baby together, even if it's just five minutes, so that she will feel a part of it and not left out.

I'm glad you've had a good week (meeting handsome Texans! You just watch out!); after a bumpy start so have we. Roly went away to Newcastle for just one night, and I missed him more than I would have thought possible, but it gave me the opportunity I needed to talk to Cherry and make my confession. When Roly came back the next day, he'd brought her the most beautiful china ornament that he found in an antique shop. I told him that it's far too valuable to give to a child, especially one as clumsy as Cherry, but he insisted that he had bought it especially for her. She mumbled her thanks—not quite as ungraciously as usual—and seemed reasonably pleased with it. She put it away very carefully on a high shelf, but it's only a matter of time before it gets smashed to smithereens.

I sometimes wonder whether Roly is trying too hard. Might it not be better if he gave her tit for tat and treated her with the same contempt as she treats him? Unfortunately—or fortunately—it's just not in his nature. He is a gentle and caring person, and I'm afraid that Cherry rides roughshod over him. I'm hoping that the baby will bring out the softer side of her nature. If she has one!

No, that's not fair. On the whole she has a very bubbly personality and can be quite warm and loving when she chooses. I remember after Greg and I first split up that she was incredibly supportive. I couldn't have asked for a better daughter. It's just that at the moment, events are rather conspiring to bring out the worst in her.

On Saturday she wanted to go to a sleepover at a friend's house, and we had an argument when I wouldn't let her. Roly says I should have taken the chance, but he hasn't seen the girl's parents! The father works as a loan shark and the mother—well! The mother is something else. Huge peroxide beehive, mascara ten inches thick, mock leopardskin coat. Roly says what does it matter, but I don't want Cherry being led into bad ways and coming back here using foul language, which she is likely to do. The beehive's child swears like a trooper.

Anyway, to make up for not letting her go, we all went out for pizza and then came back to watch a video. Guess what we saw? Snow White! Did you ever see it when you were a kid? I adored it—and still do! Cherry was sulking at first, but afterward she went into the hall to telephone one of her friends, and I heard her laughing, so she was obviously happy, which is something she hasn't always been lately.

Cherry's desperately looking forward to staying with Greg for a few days during October break. I just hope he doesn't let her down. Originally she was going to go for the whole week, but surprise, surprise! He can't get the time off. Funny he could spend two weeks in Florida back in July and is going off skiing for another two weeks at Christmas, but he can't spare just one week to be with his own daughter.

I know I mustn't run her dad down in front of her, but the temptation is sometimes very strong. Happily on this occasion, bless him, Roly stepped in before I could open my big mouth and say something that I might have regretted. I wouldn't want to poison Cherry's mind against her dad. I won't say she regards him as a god, exactly, but he is certainly far higher in the popularity stakes than poor Roly. On the other hand, I do believe I have detected a slight softening in her attitude just recently. I'm keeping my fingers crossed!

Please report on handsome Texans.

Love,

Patsy

Monday

He's still shoving these cards under my door. I really hate the thought of him creeping around while I'm asleep. I just keep throwing them away. I'm still on strike and so the wastebasket has spilled over, and everything is dusty except for the crinoline lady on her top shelf. I'm too scared to dust her because she's fragile, so I blow on her very gently. Maybe if she gets dirty, I can give her a bubble bath and use the hair dryer.

Terrible fight with Mum this morning when I

arrived downstairs in T-shirt, leggings, and my Doc Martens. She screamed, "You can't wear those clothes to school! You go back upstairs and change immediately!" "Into what?" I said, "It may have escaped your memory, but we don't happen to have any uniform at this school; we can wear whatever we like, and right now everybody is wearing T-shirts and tights and Doc Martens."

Mum said not to take that tone with her. (What tone? What is she talking about?) She said she didn't care what other people were wearing. She wouldn't have her daughter go to school looking like some kind of big-footed monster. I said, "That's very big-footist." And she snarled, "Never mind the smart mouth! I have spoken and it's final. How can you expect to do any serious learning in that ridiculous getup?"

Mum is incredibly stubborn. I said, "Well, then, how can you expect to have a serious baby, wearing those ridiculous overalls?" which is what she has taken to wearing now that her secret is out. I said, "I bet the queen didn't wear overalls when she was having babies." Mum started to get all red and hot, but old Slimey laughed and said, "She's got you there!" almost as if he were on my side against Mum.

I met the Skinbag at the school gates and asked her what the sleepover was like. She said it was fun and that *When Harry Met Sally* was even better the second time around and why wouldn't my mum let me go? I told her it was because of Gemma's brother saying "That Word" and Mum thinking I might start saying it, and the Melon agreed that mothers could be a real drag. She said that right at this moment, hers was being even more of a drag than usual, which I found hard to believe, since the Melon's mum is really cool. She would never make promises and then break them. Like if she said the Melon could have a dog, then she'd let her have a dog. She's already got one, of course, but if she'd asked if she could have another, or choose a video or whatever, Skinny's mum would let her. So I said, "How is she being a drag?" but the Melon wouldn't tell me. She just said, "Behaving like a teenager."

I don't see anything particularly draggy about that.

When I got home from school, Mum started in on the baby again. She was wondering whether it was going to be a boy or a girl and trying to get me to say which I'd prefer. I wouldn't prefer either! I don't want to know about the beastly baby. I hope it never comes out!

Tuesday

Boiled organs and baked toenails for lunch. One of the boys said that they were organs. Male organs. He fished some out and made disgusting patterns with them on the table. Boys like doing that kind of thing. Skinny said she thought the toenails might in fact be potato skins, but who wants to eat potato skins? What happened to the insides of the potatoes? Skinny says we'll probably get to have those tomorrow, all lumpy and nasty.

Got into trouble with Mrs. James today because she said I was rude to her. I wasn't! She accused me of passing notes, and it was John Lloyd and Steven Carter; I just happened to pick one up off the floor for them. Mrs. James said, "There are other ways of letting me know that you have been falsely accused. There is no need to be aggressive."

I complained to Skinny Melon about it afterward, and Skinny said, "Well, you were aggressive. You always are, these days. People hardly dare open their mouths because you might jump on them."

I can't help it. I feel aggressive. I feel like screaming sometimes. It's living with Mum and Slimey and this baby that Mum's carrying around with her. That's what's doing it.

I keep remembering when Dad was here, before he and Mum started fighting. I was happy then. I haven't been happy since Mum and Dad split up. I hate them all!

Wednesday

Got into more trouble. Miss Bradley, this time. We were playing basketball, and she pulled me aside for running with the ball when I wasn't. She just thought I was because someone barged into me. I explained this to her, as politely as I could. I said, "Excuse me, but you've made a mistake," and she instantly jumped down my throat and yelled that she was sick and tired of what she called my "attitude." Why does everyone keep nagging at me all the time? I can't wait till I can go and stay with Dad.

I was so frustrated about Miss Bradley screaming at me and Skinny being distant after telling me I was aggressive that I decided I wasn't going to stay in for lunch today like we're supposed to. For one thing, I couldn't stand the thought of having to eat the insides of yesterday's potatoes, and for another, I saw Skinny going off with Avril Roper and Uchenna Jackson. I hopped out through the gates when no one was looking and walked to town. I got some chips and a bottle of Coke and headed up the road to the station, which is where the cab company is that Dad used to work for after he'd been laid off.

Lots of the same drivers were there and they remembered me and asked how I was doing and how Dad was liking his new job. They're much more fun than the people Mum and Slimey know. All of Mum and Slimey's friends are either writers or publishers or something else having to do with books. Books are all they ever talk about. They're always pushing them on me. "Here's a copy of my new book for you, Cherry." "Here's a copy of a book we've just published, Cherry." "Here's a copy of a book I thought you might like, Cherry."

And then I'm expected to sit down and read them and say what I think of them, which most of the time isn't much, only I'm not allowed to say so for fear of being rude or hurting their feelings. It's not that I don't like books; it's just that I don't like *their* books. They're all so babyish! I'm more into horror. Mum and Slimey are horrified (ho-ho!), but I say what's wrong with reading something scary? They don't seem to realize that I've grown out of all their kiddy crud.

When it was time to go back to school, one of the drivers, named Ivy, said she'd take me in her cab. We talked a bit on the way, and Ivy asked me how I liked my mum's new husband. I was glad she didn't say "your new dad" 'cause I can't stand it when people do that. So I made a face, and Ivy said, "Tough going?" And then she told me how it had happened to her when she was about my age and how she'd thought she'd never get used to her mum having a new husband, "Never!" but how in the end she had, and, "Now we're the best of friends."

I know Ivy was only trying to be helpful, but I'm afraid it's not going to work out like that for me. I still have my real dad, even if he does live miles away. It was different for Ivy because her real dad was not a very nice person. In fact Ivy said he was "a down-right *******." (I have to put stars for the word Ivy used, since it's not the sort of word I wish to record in this diary.) I told her that my dad is the best dad in the world and that I'm going to visit with him soon. I said that I'm really looking forward to it. Ivy said, "Well, have a good time, but don't expect too much."

I don't know why she said that. I didn't have a chance to ask her because we had already reached the school gates. Skinny was milling about nearby with Avril and Uchenna. You should have seen their faces when they realized who was in the cab!

They couldn't have been more surprised if I'd stepped out of a Rolls-Royce. Skinny shrieked, "Where have you been?" It was just my bad luck that Mrs. James happened to be passing at that particular moment and also wanted to know where I had been.

I told her I'd been visiting my dad's old colleagues and she said, "You do know you're not supposed to leave the premises at lunchtime without permission?" and I said yes, which was a dumb thing to say. I should have said no, though I don't expect ignorance is any

Mrs. James looking like a Popsicle.

defense, and she said, "Very well, Cherry," all frozen and unsmiling like a Popsicle with the color sucked out of it.

I have to go and see her tomorrow, first thing after assembly.

I know what that means. It means she's going to bawl me out and threaten to tell Mum. I don't care! It was worth it. I'm glad I went. I don't see what right they have to keep making all these rules and regulations anyway. Nobody ever asks kids what we want. Grown-ups do just whatever they like. Get divorced. Marry creeps. Have babies. Whatever.

Thursday

Went to see Mrs. James. Actually she was pretty nice. She said that "this sort of behavior" couldn't continue but that she didn't want to have to write to Mum unless I absolutely forced her to, and then she said, "Did you ever think about my suggestion for keeping a diary?" and I said yes, I was doing it, and she asked me if it was helping, but without prying into the reason why I might need help, which is what lots of teachers would have done. So to please her, I said I thought perhaps it was, just a little, and she told me to keep writing in it because it could only be a good thing.

I hope she's right. I do like putting things down in writing. I can say lots of stuff that I couldn't say to anyone else, not even the Melon—who is back being friends with me again. It seems that we can't survive without each other.

I stayed in school at lunchtime and dutifully ate yuck. It made me feel sick. I feel sick most of the time now, what with eating yuck and Mum and Slimey going on and on about the blessed baby. Even the names they have come up with are yuck. If it's a boy, it's going to be Bernard . . . Bernard Butter. If it's a girl, they're going to name her Belinda. Mum says she likes what she called the allitration.

Alliteration. (Just looked it up in the dictionary.) This means having two letters the same. B and B. Like bed and breakfast. Or bread and butter.

I just thought of a joke. If it's a girl they could call it Bredan, which is Brenda mixed up. Ha-ha! That is a Slimey joke. I'll suggest it to them.

Friday

Dog's vomit and earwax, with crusty bits on top. I didn't ask anyone what it was supposed to be. I think it's better not to know. I just held my breath and swallowed. I am seriously thinking of taking up Mum's offer of vegetarian sandwiches. I would if it weren't for old Slimey. I hate the thought of him crowing because he's won me over. If I decide to do it, it will be out of sheer desperation and a desire not to be poisoned. Nothing whatsoever to do with him.

When I got in at dinnertime, he was there, which I didn't expect because he'd gone off earlier to bore some more poor little kids. So I told them my idea for calling the baby Bredan and Mum stupidly said, "Oh, you mean like Bredon Hill? But that's pronounced Breedon." Slime got it. He got it straightaway. He said, "Bredan Butter! Brilliant!" and promptly started to sketch a loaf of bread on the kitchen table with his felt-tip pen that he always keeps handy in case sudden inspiration comes to him. Mum said, "Oh! Yes. I see. Then we'd have a Roll and Butter and a Bread and Butter. Clever!"

Slimey said, "Yes, and if we had another one we could call it Toastan." I have been trying without success to think of other things that go with butter. All I can think of is T. K. Cann-Butter and Chris P. Bredan Butter. But they're not very good.

I suppose you can have Saul T. Butter. That's not bad.

A woman up the street who just moved in has asked Mum if I'd like to go and have tea tomorrow with her daughter because her daughter is the same age as me and doesn't yet know anyone. Mum said that I would! I don't particularly want to go and have tea with this girl. Her name is Sereena, which I know is not her fault, and her last name is Swaddle, which again I know she can't be blamed for. Sereena Swaddle. That is alliteration. Mum says it is "unfortunate," but why she should think it's any more unfortunate than Belinda or Bernard Butter is beyond me.

Skinny called later to know if I wanted to go swimming with her tomorrow afternoon, and I had to say that I was having tea with this Sereena person. Skinny said, "Who?" and I said, "Sereena Swaddle," and she said, "You're joking!" I said that I only wished I was. I went back to Mum and said, "Do I have to do this?" and she said, "Oh, Cherry, just once! It won't hurt you. She's a sweet little thing. I know you'll like her."

When Mum said "sweet little thing," old Slime caught my eye and made a face. And I'd gone and made one back before I could stop myself. I don't think I ought to do that. It's like we ganged up together against Mum. Mum must have sensed it because she said, "You can laugh! It's nice to know there are still some sweet little things . . . they don't all clump around in army boots, shouting four-letter words and watching ghastly horror movies."

I just thought of something else that could go with butter. P. Nutt-Butter. Now that's a good one!

Saturday

Ha! So much for Mum not letting me go to Gemma's sleepover in case she corrupted me. I went to have tea with the Sereena person this afternoon.

The sweet little thing who doesn't swear or watch horror movies. I can see why Mum thought she was a sweet little thing. It's only because she has a sweet little face. She also has long blond hair and rose-pink cheeks and eyes the size of satellite dishes and blue as whatever's blue. The sky. Forget-me-nots. Saffires. Rather revolting, really. At least, I think so. But it's what grown-ups like.

So anyway, we had tea and her mum was there and she's sort of . . . frothy. All fizzing and bubbling like Andrew's Fruit Salts that Dad used to take for his acid indigestion. She kept giggling and saying things like "Oh, Reena." (That's what she calls her. Double yuck.) "Oh, Reena, isn't this fun! You've found a friend already!" But I don't know whether I want to be her friend. I like to choose my own friends, and besides, I've got Skinny.

Afterward we went up to her room, and she said, "What do you want to do?" And I said, "Whatever you want to do." And she said, "Would you like to see some pictures of people having babies?"

I lied and said, "I've seen pictures of people having babies."

"All right," she said. "What about pictures of people completely naked?" I said, "Where would you get pictures of people naked?" and she said her best friend, Sharon, where she used to live, had torn them out of a magazine and photocopied them for her. She said some of them were really gross. "Do you want to have a look?"

I was tempted to say yes because I thought it would get Mum back for not letting me go to Gemma's sleepover, and it would be a new experience, and I do believe in having new experiences, but really, to be honest, I didn't want to. I mean that sort of thing could screw you up for life, and I'd like to grow up to be reasonably normal.

Sereena said, "Oh, well, if you don't think you can take it, I'll tell you some jokes instead, shall I?" And before I could stop her she told me all these jokes that her friend Sharon had told her, which I won't repeat in here because this is a diary and not a reseptikle for filth.

Pause while I look in the dictionary. That word is spelled *receptacle*. And *saffire* is spelled *sapphire*. I'm very good at spelling, on the whole. Mrs. James said to me the other day (before we had our little talk), "Your spelling and punctuation are excellent, Cherry." On the other hand, I cannot understand numbers, which is what Mr. Fisher, who teaches math, calls "a decided drawback." Mum can't understand numbers, either, and neither can Slimey Roland, but it doesn't matter to them since they have jobs where figures are not important. Mr. Fisher says that anyone who is not numerate, meaning anyone that can't add or subtract, will have a hard time in the twenty-first century. He says we must come to terms with technology or perish.

Computers are technology, and I'm not very good with computers, either. I don't know what I'll end up doing. Sweeping the streets, I expect. I don't think I'll be able to work with books like Mum does because there probably won't be any books left, just CD-ROMs, or whatever they are. And I don't think there will be people drawing pictures of elves, either. It will all be done by computer, and people such as

me in the future

myself will be left behind like empty bottles along the beach.

I tried talking about this with Sereena, thinking I would find out what kind of things she likes other than telling rude jokes, but I couldn't have a decent conversation with her as I can with the Melon. All Sereena can do is bat her satellite dishes and giggle. Of course the Melon is a bit of an intellectual; I mean, she has a real brain. Sereena's brain, if she has one, is about the size of a pea.

When I got home, Mum said, "There! That wasn't so bad, was it?" I told her it was "enlightening" and she said, "Why? What did you do?" I said, "Read porno magazines and told dirty jokes." Mum laughed. She thought it was really funny. "No, seriously," she said.

I said that seriously we had discussed what we thought would happen in the twenty-first century, and I had come to the sad conclusion that far from being a rock star or a judge, I would most likely end up living in a cardboard box because I was not numerate and couldn't make friends with computers the way some people could. Skinny, for example, and Sereena. Mum told me not to be so pessimistic. She said, "You're like me, you're into words." I said yes, but there won't be any words. Just computer-speak. Mum said, "Oh, what a bleak picture!" I said, "Yes, it is, but I think we have to face facts."

Mum doesn't want to face them. She says that if it's going to be a world without books and pictures, then she'd sooner not be here. Slimey didn't play any part in this conversation. He was upstairs finishing some more elves to meet his deadline, meaning (I think) that his publishers will sue him if he hasn't drawn the right number by a certain date.

It was nice being on my own with Mum, even if our conversation was rather grim. At least she didn't mention the baby, which is now sticking out in front of her like a huge sack of potatoes.

← Mum

← baby

She asked me the other day if I'd like to feel her stomach, but I said no, thank you very much.

Tomorrow I'm going to stay with Dad. Hooray, hooray, hooray! Three whole days without Slimey Roland! No more stupid jokes, no more stupid cards! I can go to bed at night and know that nobody is going to come along to shove stuff under my door while I'm asleep.

Dad is picking me up in his car. He's driving all the way from Southampton and is arriving at about nine o'clock, so I must be up early. I'm going to set my alarm. Fortunately, I've already packed my suitcase; I did it this morning with Mum's help. She kept saying things like, "Well, you won't need all that much, now that it's only for a few days." She just refuses to accept that Dad is an important person. There is a great deal depending on Dad, and he has to be prepared to work long hours. It's not his fault. I do wish Mum could see this.

I'm going to take my diary with me just in case, but I expect I'll be too busy to write anything in it. The next three days are going to be ACTION PACKED!

141 Arethusa Road
London W5
25 October

Dearest Carol,

I can't believe it! A Texan called Dwayne? Is this a real name??? He sure does sound hunky!

No, no, no, I'm only joking! In all seriousness, I'm really glad you've found someone to have fun with. You deserve it. Enjoy! But full reports, please. I am consumed with vulgar curiosity.

Cherry has suggested that if the baby is a girl we should call her Bredan . . . get it? She is picking up this sort of humor from Roly. But I was so pleased that she feels able to make jokes about it. It shows she's been thinking.

Yesterday she went over to have tea with a new little girl who has just moved into our neighborhood. I call her a little girl because although she is the same age as Cherry, she is most delightfully quaint and old-fashioned! She actually wears a big red bow in her hair and shiny shoes with ankle straps. It takes me right back! Cherry, by contrast, is into all this heavy grunge gear and walks around looking like something that's crawled out of a garbage heap. I feel it would do her good to make friends with someone like Sereena.

At the moment she isn't here because she has gone off to spend a few days with Greg. There are times when I could cheerfully strangle that man! He had arranged to pick her up at about nine o'clock and she was all ready and waiting down in the hall with her suitcase, wearing her best clothes (i.e., the grungiest ones she could find), and by 10:30, when he still hadn't arrived, I called Southampton and got his new wife, Rosemary, and she says, "Oh, yeah, he just left about ten minutes ago." Of course by then the roads were busy, which meant he didn't get here until lunchtime.

It really is too bad. Poor Cherry sitting there waiting like some faithful hound and this irresponsible oaf not even bothering to call and let us know! Cherry was almost in tears. When he finally turned up, she went catapulting into his arms and it was all kissy-kissy, huggy-huggy. I expect I ought to have found it touching, but the truth is I was too angry. Also, I suppose, if I am to be honest, I was a bit hurt at her being so obviously eager to get away from us. Roly says, "Come on, it's her dad. She hasn't seen him for six months," and I know that I mustn't be jealous but it seems so unfair! He comes breezing in, three hours late, and she's all over him with never so much as a backward glance for me and Roly. I offered the fool a cup of coffee (I wasn't going to offer him lunch!), but I could tell that Cherry just wanted to be off.

Oh, aren't I sour and crabby! But I do dread her returning home full of discontent, telling me how wonderful it is at her dad's and how horrible it is here. They're bound to spoil her rotten; it's only to be expected. And it will never occur to her that they've only had her for three days, while we have her permanently. She's a bright child but not always the easiest to get along with, which I know is partly my fault. My fault and Greg's. Our getting divorced has been difficult for her. I keep telling myself that I must make allowances.

Oh, but she can be so difficult! Roly felt that he would like to give her something as a going-away present. A little something to take with her. He asked me if she would like a book and I said yes; I thought a book would be an excellent idea, because one thing she does is read, even if it is mostly schlock horror. He went to such pains to find one that she would like. She is writing this diary at the moment (it's supposed to be a secret, but she lets these little remarks slip from time to time), and we suddenly remembered that wonderful book that you and I read when we were Cherry's age. I Capture the Castle.

Do you remember it? Cassandra Morton sitting on the draining board writing her journal with her feet in the sink? How we wallowed in it! So Roly combed through half the secondhand bookshops in London until he found an original copy, and he slipped it into her bedroom while she was asleep, with one of his funny little notes all done in pictures, telling her to take it with her to read while she was away, and what do you think? I've just been in there (it looks like a bomb site, but I refuse to clean it), and she left the book lying on the floor! I haven't dared to tell Roly; he would be hurt.

It sometimes seems to me that the harder Roly tries, the worse she treats him. And I have this horrible feeling that she is going to be even more impossible when she comes back from Greg's.

Children! Think twice before embarking, no matter how handsome your Texan may be!

Eagerly await news of developments from your end. Will report back from mine.

Love,

Patsy

P.S. We're going to take the opportunity to redecorate the spare bedroom for the baby while Cherry is away. We're also going to buy all the necessary paraphernalia—stroller, crib, car seat! I thought I had finished with all that. Roly is really excited. I only wish Cherry were, so that we could share it. I could really look forward to the event if I thought that she were happy.

Monday

No time to write in here yesterday so I am doing it now while Rosemary has her bath and gets ready to go out. She takes a long time to get ready, at least she did yesterday when we went for pizza. We're going out every single day that I am here! This is because Rosemary doesn't like cooking, which is all right by me. I like to go out.

Tonight we're off to an Indian restaurant, and tomorrow we are going to a Chinese one. To think that at home, we only go out about once every six months! But I expect Dad and Rosemary earn a lot more money than Mum and Slimey do, which is only right.

I met Rosemary only two times before so I don't really know her very well. I met her before she got married to Dad and once after. That was almost a year ago. Since then I have seen Dad only once when I came to Southampton for the day, but Rosemary wasn't there.

Rosemary is pretty and wears lots of makeup and hip clothes. She's younger than Mum and of course much slimmer. Even if Mum weren't having this baby, Rosemary would still be much slimmer. She and Dad go jogging every morning, and Rosemary also does aerobics. Dad has started to play squash and is not anywhere near as pudgy as when he was driving the cab.

I must say it's a great relief to be in a house—well, an apartment actually—where everything isn't geared toward a baby. There are no signs of a baby in this place, thank goodness!

It was strange at first being in an apartment after being used to a house, but now I think that I prefer the apartment. It would be sensible if everyone lived in an apartment because then there would be a lot more land where you could grow grass and trees. I think probably it's almost antisocial for people to live in houses. I'm going to say this to Slimey next time he goes on about the environment and how we are ruining it. Dad and Rosemary aren't taking up half the space that he and Mum take up! Also I enjoy everything being on one level so that you don't have to keep rushing up and down the stairs all the time. There is even an elevator where you can meet people and talk. I want to live in an apartment when I am grown up—if I'm not living in a cardboard box, that is.

I told Dad about the cardboard box, and he said that he'll buy me a computer for my Christmas present. He said, "I cannot have a daughter of mine being computer illiterate, but of course your mother has always had a tendency to be a bit of a Luddite." I said what is a Luddite and he said they are people who go around smashing machinery. I said that I didn't think Mum smashed it on purpose, she just wasn't very good with it, like, for instance, last week, she broke the handle off the washing machine and put the vacuum bag in the wrong way so that all the dust came flying out into the house.

Dad said, "Typical! And I suppose *he's* not much better?" I said, "Slimey? He's even worse!" which isn't the truth, since it was Slimey who fixed the handle of the washing machine with superglue and changed the bag in the vacuum cleaner. But it's true that neither of them knows the first thing about computers. Mum just uses her word processor like an ordinary typewriter. This used to drive Dad mad when he was living with us. He was always trying to teach her different things that she could do on it, but she wouldn't listen. She used to say, "Oh, I can't be bothered with all that!"

The ride from London to Southampton in Dad's car was great except that halfway here I started to feel carsick, which Dad said was probably because I'd gotten out of the habit of traveling by car. I said yes, Slimey always insisted on going everywhere by bus or bicycle. He said, "Like it or not, the car is here to stay," and, "You can't put the clock back." Anyway, we had to stop a couple of times so that I could get some air and then I felt good again. But I never felt carsick before. It's all Slimey's fault.

Today we went for a drive to the New Forest (I didn't get sick this time) and had lunch and then drove to a place called Lymington, which is by the sea. It was too cold to go swimming, so we just looked at it and came home again. Tomorrow Dad has to go into the office in the morning because there is a problem that only he can sort out, so Rosemary and I are meeting him for lunch and then sightseeing around Southampton where there is an old museum and an ancient wall. And of course the docks. I'm looking forward to it.

I called Mum last night to tell her that we had arrived safely (she worries about accidents), and she said, "So how are you? I suppose everything is going well?" I said that it was and that so far I was enjoying myself (though, in fact, we hadn't done very much at that point). I said, "Dad's told me I can stay till Friday if I want." He told me in the car. It was one of the first things he said. He said, "Rosemary's managed to wangle an extra two days, and I'll take off what time I can."

"That's good, isn't it?" I said to Mum. I thought she would be pleased, but she didn't sound very pleased. She just grunted and said, "If that's what you want."

"Well, I thought I might as well," I said, "now that I'm here."

"That's right," said Mum. "Make the most of it. It doesn't happen that often."

Then there was a pause and she said, "You left your book behind." I couldn't think of what she was talking about. I said, "What book?" She said, "Roly's book. The one he bought specially for you." I knew from the tone of her voice that she was upset with me. I forgot all about his book. I wouldn't have brought it anyway. What do I want to read for, when I'm with Dad?

Mum said, "It's not worth giving things to you, is it?" It is, if they're the right things, but anyway she didn't have to get all wound up about it because I'm also pretty wound up, if she really wants to know. What I'm wound up about is the thought of Slime actually opening my door and creeping into my room while I'm asleep. I don't think he has any right to do that. He's not my dad. But if I'd said so to Mum, she'd only get defensive, like she always does where Slimey is concerned, and I didn't want to argue with her over the telephone. So I just said, "Look, I'm sorry, I forgot," and she said, "Yes, of course, you left in such a rush!" I think she was being sarcastic. It was the way she used to get with Dad. I hope she's not going to start in on me. It's nice and peaceful here. I don't want Mum calling up and making trouble.

Tuesday

The museum was very interesting. It's called The Wool House and is full of relics from the Napoleonic days. French prisoners were kept there, and you can still see their initials where they'd carved them into the wooden beams. It gave me a strange feeling to think of prisoners doing that all those years ago and me standing here today looking at them. It made me wonder if people in two hundred years' time would stand and look at something I'd done, like, for instance, I once carved my initials on a tree and the date. I imagined a girl like me finding it and wondering who I was and what had become of me. It was creepy but at the same time comforting, to know that you have made your mark and will leave something behind.

Tomorrow we're supposed to go to Portsmouth to see the *Victory*, which is the ship that Admiral Nelson sailed in.

Wednesday

We couldn't go to Portsmouth today because Dad was needed at the office again. Well, Rosemary and I could have gone, but it wouldn't have been the same without Dad. She said we could go if I liked, but I said I'd rather wait for him and she said she would, too. She said as a matter of fact, there were things she had to do, like hemming an evening dress she is making for herself for a fancy dinner party that she and Dad are going to on Friday night. She asked if I would mind if she stayed in and did that?

Of course I said no, and she said I could do whatever I wanted, watch the television or go for a walk. She said there was a park just up the street, so I went, but it wasn't very interesting, no dogs to play with and nothing really to do, so I came back again and watched as she used her sewing machine and I wondered why Mum couldn't make her own clothes.

Mum is absolutely useless; she can't even sew on buttons properly. I also wondered why Mum couldn't wear the sort of clothes that Rosemary wears. Her evening dress, for instance, is completely incredible—showing lots of cleavage.

Rosemary in ← her dress.

I have never seen Mum wear anything like that.

We were supposed to be meeting Dad again for lunch but he phoned to say he wasn't going to be able to make it (some very important Americans have come over and he has to be with them). I could see that Rosemary was put off by this. I think she didn't know what to do with me. She said, "I guess we'd better find some way of amusing you. There's a zoo over on the Common. Would you like to go to the zoo?" I said that I was sorry but I didn't believe in zoos, I think it's cruel to keep animals locked up in small spaces, and she said, "Oh, you're one of those, are you? I'm surprised you're not a vegetarian." I said, "I probably am going to be, soon," and she made a face, as if I'd announced that I was going to have all my teeth pulled out or my hands chopped off.

Since I wouldn't go to the zoo, she suggested the movies. She said, "There's bound to be something suitable for children." I told her that I didn't normally watch things that were suitable for children. She said, "Well, I'm not taking you to some awful horror movie, if that's what you're after." I said she didn't need to take me anywhere; I'm accustomed to entertaining myself, and so we ate some soup and a can of peaches in the kitchen, and she went back to her evening dress, and I came in here to write in my diary.

It's now three o'clock, and Dad still isn't back. Rosemary thinks he probably won't be home until about seven, when we can all go out for a meal. It's hard to think of what to do until then. I don't really want to watch television because it's in the same room where Rosemary's doing her sewing, and she's got the radio on. I've looked for some books but there don't seem to be any. I should have brought the one that Slimey got for me, but how was I to know that Dad would have to work?

Maybe I could go into Southampton and shop.

Thursday

I don't think Rosemary will ever have a baby. She doesn't seem to like children very much. I said to her yesterday that I was going to go shopping in Southampton, and she said, "You can't go by yourself, you'll get lost." And then she heaved this big irritable sort of sigh and said, "I suppose I'll have to come with you." We couldn't go by car because Dad had taken it, so we had to go by bus, which I'm quite used to on account of Slimey not driving. But I don't think Rosemary is, since she kept tapping her foot and looking at her watch and trying to find out from the timetable when the next bus was due. It made me feel guilty, as if I ought to have stayed quietly indoors, but it's just as well I hadn't because Dad didn't get home until almost nine o'clock, by which time I had read two horror books I bought (*Scream and You're Dead* and *House of Horror*) and was absolutely starving.

Today was a better day. We went to Portsmouth to see the *Victory*. Dad and I went; Rosemary didn't come. The *Victory* was fascinating, and it was nice being with Dad on my own. He was more like I remember him from the old days. When he is with Rosemary, he's different. It's hard to describe it. He acts like one of those men who wear ponytails and drive around in fast cars, talking on cell phones. What Mum and Slimey call yuppies.

When we got back from Portsmouth, Dad said I could go to the video shop and make my choice, as he had promised me. I was tempted to choose a horror film, just to show Rosemary that if I wanted to watch it, I could, but then I thought maybe if I picked that, Dad would be like Mum and break his promise, so I picked instead a film called *Strictly Ballroom,* which is all about ballroom dancing. To be honest, I'm not really into dancing, but Skinny Melon had told me it had this gorgeous guy in it, and she was right, it did! I'm now seriously thinking of asking Mum if I can learn ballroom dancing. Imagine meeting a guy like that! (Some hopes!)

Dad and Rosemary, unfortunately, got bored. Rosemary went and sat over on the other side of the room and did her sewing, and Dad went and took a bath, so I was left on my own. I didn't really mind, I suppose, though it's nicer when other people enjoy what you enjoy. I think Mum would like the movie. It's her sort of thing. Next time we get a video I'll tell her to get that one.

Tomorrow I'm going home. I'm trying to remember the things that I have seen and done so that I can tell Mum. I've been to the New Forest. I've been to the sea. I've been to the museum. I've seen the *Victory*. I've seen *Strictly Ballroom*. I have eaten: one Italian meal, one Indian meal, one Chinese meal, one French meal, and one American meal (hamburgers, only I had a veggie burger, thinking of Slimey and dead things in the fridge). I suppose that's quite a lot of things to have seen and done in five days.

Later

Dad and Rosemary just had an argument about who is going to drive me back tomorrow. I heard them when I went to the bathroom. (I've noticed that in an apartment, you can often hear people talking. It's not as private as in a house.) I heard Rosemary say, "She's your daughter!" and then Dad said something that I couldn't catch, but I think it was about needing to go into the office again, and Rosemary said, "I am not driving her all the way to London."

I'm glad she isn't driving me. I don't think I could bear it, and I don't expect she could either.

Friday

Now I'm back home. I had to come by train because Rosemary refused to drive me and Dad had to go into the office. It's a bit of a drawback in some ways, having a father who is so important. I'm glad, of course, that he is important, but I would have liked it better if he had been there more of the time, since it wasn't much fun when he wasn't. I don't feel that comfortable with Rosemary. I think she would have preferred that I hadn't come at all.

I called Mum before we left to tell her what time my train was getting in. She was furious, I could tell. She said, "Train? All by yourself?" And I said yes, because Dad had to work. "Oh, does he?" she said. "Where is he? Let me speak to him!" I didn't want her to, but she started to shout. She shouted, "You put him on the phone!" It was so loud that Dad heard it and came and took the receiver from me. He said, "Hello? Pat?" quite pleasantly, I thought, but it soon developed into one of their fights.

I think Mum must have asked him why I couldn't stay till Saturday and come back by car because Dad sort of twisted his lips in a way that said, "I'm being very patient, but don't push me," and informed her that, "Rosemary and I happen to have a business dinner party that we must go to this evening. It's not something we can get out of, nor would we wish to. All right?"

I don't know what Mum said after that because I couldn't bear to listen anymore. Why does everything always get so awful when Mum and Dad talk to each other? I wish they hadn't! It ruined the end of my trip.

Dad and Rosemary both came to the station with me. I would rather it had just been Dad, but at least Rosemary stayed in the car, which meant I was able to say good-bye to Dad on my own. He said, "We've had fun this week, haven't we? We must do it again—and not leave it so long next time." I said that maybe I could come at Christmas, but Dad said unfortunately that wouldn't be possible because he and Rosemary had already arranged to go with friends to Austria for a ski trip. I didn't want to suggest that maybe I could go with them because I don't think Rosemary would approve. Then I had a bright idea and said, "Parents' Evening! You could come to Parents' Evening!" Dad said he thought that was an excellent idea and if I let him know when it was, he would definitely be there. He said, "That's a promise!"

We had a while to wait, so Dad bought me some magazines and another horror book. Unlike Mum and Slimey, he didn't say anything about me reading horror stories but said it looked exciting and that it ought to keep me on the edge of my seat all the way to London. As it happens, I can't read very well on trains because they jerk up and down, but I didn't say so to Dad. Instead I said that I would find out the date of Parents' Evening and let him know. He said, "Make sure you do!" and then it was time to say good-bye and for me to get on the train.

This was the first time that I have ever been on a long train ride by myself. I kept worrying how I would know when we reached London, which was stupid because London is where the train stops. It doesn't go anywhere else. And then I worried about leaving my seat to go to the bathroom in case I couldn't find my way back or someone stole my things. And then when I absolutely had to go or else I'd burst, it was one of those bathrooms where you have to press buttons to get in and more buttons to close the door, and I was terrified I wouldn't be able to get out again. But of course I did. I expect if I got used to traveling on my own, it would be all right.

Another thing I worried about was what I would do if I got to London and couldn't see Mum or Slimey, but Slimey was there, waiting for me, looking all Slimeyish in a jogging suit and ratty old sneakers.

He gave me a big hug and kiss, and I let him, which normally I wouldn't have done because normally it would revolt me, but I was just so relieved to see him. He said, "I'm sorry Butter Pat couldn't come, but she has an appointment at the clinic." (Meaning the prenatal clinic, where all the pregnant women go to make sure they're having healthy babies and not

Slimey at the station.

babies that have things wrong with them.) He said he knew that he was second best but "hopefully better than nothing."

I felt sort of sorry for him when he said this. I also felt a bit mean about leaving his book behind, especially since I was clutching my horror book. I explained that Dad had bought me the book and that I hadn't left his behind on purpose; I'd simply forgotten to pack it, like I'd also forgotten to pack my toothbrush (this was a lie, but I said it to make him feel better). I said that I wished I had taken his book because I'd had to go out and buy myself some, and I promised that I would read his next. Slimey said, "I'm afraid you won't find it very exciting after your diet of horror. I probably made a mistake in choosing it." He sounded really sad, as if it mattered to him that I might not find his book exciting. I said that I would definitely read it and let him know.

When we got home Mum was there. I'd forgotten how enormous she looks after Rosemary. She asked me if I'd had a good time, and I said, "Wonderful," because it would have been disloyal to Dad to have said anything else. Mum said, "Well, there's nothing very wonderful on this end, but we can go up to the video shop and get a movie, if you like." I said, "Can I choose?" and Mum said, "Yes, but you know the rules."

So I chose *Strictly Ballroom,* and I was right: Mum loved it! So did Slime. Mum said it was a "good old-fashioned movie with no sex and no violence," and

Slime surprised everyone—well, he surprised me, but I think Mum as well—by saying that he used to be a champion tango dancer, and to prove it, he jumped up and pulled me into the middle of the room and taught me how to do it. He was really good. So now I know how to tango!

Me and Slimey tango.

Saturday

He's still shoving cards under my door, and I still don't like it, but I suppose he's only doing it to be friendly. Imagine being so desperate to be liked!

After breakfast I called the Melon, and we arranged to meet at the top of my street and go shopping together. She wanted to know what it was like at Dad's, so I said the same as I said to Mum, that it was wonderful. I told her all the things I'd done and then asked her what she'd done.

Skinny said she hadn't done anything at all. She

sounded a bit down in the dumps so I asked her what was the matter, and at first she said nothing, but then she said that her mum had met this man where she works and his name was Melvin and that he was weird. I was going to say that he couldn't possibly be any weirder than Slime, but for some reason, I didn't. I don't know why. I said, "Maybe she just has bad taste in men but it doesn't really matter as long as she's not going to marry him." Skinny said rather fiercely that of course she wasn't going to marry him; he was just a boyfriend. I said, "So what's the problem?" and she said there wasn't one except that she couldn't stand the sight of him. Then she cheered up and said she wanted to go and buy a new pair of leggings with some money that he'd given her. I said, "Weird Melvin?" and she giggled and said, "He's trying to get on my good side!"

I really don't know what she's complaining about.

When I got home, I found that Slime had finished the pond. I have to admit that it's neat. It will be especially nice in the summer, with water lilies. It's not quite ready for the fish, but next week we're going to go buy some. I'm refusing to be too enthusiastic because if I am, it will make Mum think I've forgiven her for breaking her promise about the dog, which I most certainly have not.

I would still like a dog more than anything else in the world. Far more than a computer, though naturally I wouldn't say this to Dad. A computer will prevent me from living in a cardboard box (maybe—maybe not), but a dog would bring cheer and comfort into my gloomy life. I could play with it and take it for walks and feed it and brush it and cuddle it and talk to it, and it could even sleep in bed with me. Oh, why does Slimey Roland have to suffer from stupid allergies!

My dear Carol,

Your Texan sounds more divine every time you write! Photo, please. I picture him as being a cross between Steve McQueen and the Incredible Hulk . . . Roly can't even begin to compete, but I don't care. I love him to death!

Well, Cherry has come back from Southampton, and just as I feared, they have spoiled her rotten. She informs me that Dad took her out to dinner every single night. Dad took her to have an Indian meal; Dad took her to have a Chinese meal; Dad took her to have pizza; Dad took her to have oysters and champagne (so she says); Dad took her to see the Victory; Dad took her to the New Forest. I swear I'll scream if she tells me once more the wonderful time she had with Dad!

Dad is a rat. He obviously had a guilty conscience because when she got to his place, he told her that she could stay till Friday, but then I spoke with him early Friday morning, and he said he was sending her home by train because he had to go into the office. When I asked why she couldn't stay over until Saturday, he had the nerve to tell me that he and Rosemary are going to a dinner party—a dinner party, my dear!—which they certainly didn't intend to cancel on Cherry's behalf. So she ended up being shuffled onto the train like an unwanted package and sent back to us. Of course that isn't the way she sees it. She just thinks that Greg is enormously important and that the office can't function without him. He's just a computer programmer!

According to Cherry, he has promised to buy her a computer for Christmas, but I'll believe that when I see it.

I suppose it's overprotective to worry about an eleven-year-old girl traveling by herself from Southampton to Waterloo, but I kept having these terrible visions of all the things that could happen to her. A mother's mind is like a museum of horrors . . . I had to send Roly off to meet her because I was due at the clinic for a checkup. He tells me she was cheerful, her normal ebullient self, so she obviously didn't worry. I was the one to do that.

I asked about Rosemary, hoping to hear how ugly/ stupid/fat/useless/generally disagreeable she was, but it appears that she's thin as a rake, ravishingly beautiful, dresses like a fashion model, makes her own clothes, and is a hardheaded career woman. This, at least, is what I gather. What Cherry actually said, in a sarcastic tone, was that "She's never likely to have a baby," which is simply a snide way of having a go at me. I suppose she blames the baby for my not meeting her at the station. It wouldn't occur to her to blame Greg for putting her on the train in the first place!

Oh, what a moaning minnie I have become. I don't mean to be, but there's only three months to go, and she still shows no real signs of softening her attitude. I tried to show her what we'd done in the spare bedroom, but she made it very obvious that she didn't want to know. She is so full of "Dad" and what it's like at Dad's place—she even got on Roly's case today for living in a house and not an apartment. It seems it is now environmentally irresponsible to live in a house. Dad could live in one if he wanted—he's so rich and important he could live anywhere—but he chooses to live in an apartment so as not to waste land.

If you believe that, you'll believe anything! I don't know how Roly puts up with her. He has the patience of a saint.

Lots of love from your harassed,

Patsy

Sunday

Mum showed me today what they've done to the spare bedroom while I've been away. The walls are dead white with little painted teddy bears and beach balls and space rockets running along the border. Oh, and elves, of course! Elves all over the place.

Roly's sappy paintings

Mum said, "What do you think?" and I said, "I don't remember having this when I was a baby," meaning it was really nice and the sort of thing that a baby would like, but Mum took it the wrong way and snapped, "That's because you weren't lucky enough to have Roly for a father!"

She is really touchy these days. I can't seem to do anything right.

Monday

I said to Skinny Melon today that I didn't think my system could stand much more poisoning from school lunches. She said that she didn't think hers could either. She was absolutely positive that she'd found a worm on her plate, and she showed it to Mrs. James, and Mrs. James looked at it and told her not to be silly; it was "just a bit of grissle." (Gristle?) But as Skinny said, even if you believe her—which she did not—you don't pay for lunch just to be given bits of gristle. (I think this is the way it's spelled.) And as I said, it's not very nice to think you're chewing on pieces of dead animal anyway, whether it's pieces of worm or pieces of lamb.

Skinny didn't seem so sure about this until I pointed out to her that she wouldn't want to eat Lulu, would she, and she went white and said no of course she wouldn't. Then I said so what was the difference between eating Lulu and eating a lamb, and she said that she thought there was one, but she couldn't think of what it was.

We talked about it for a bit, and in the end, she agreed that if she saw a lamb in a field, she wouldn't want to kill it, and it was only the fact that it came disguised and not looking like a lamb that made her able to eat it. I said, "I bet if someone gave you a whole raw lamb to cook you wouldn't ever eat lamb again," and she really didn't have any arguments left.

So then I said that I was seriously thinking of becoming a vegetarian, and Skinny said that she was, too. I said, "When shall we do it?" and she thought about it a bit and said, "In the spring?" I said, "Why then and not now?" and she said because of the holidays. She said they always have roast turkey at Christmas and she didn't think she could live without roast turkey. Not this Christmas. Maybe next Christmas when her taste buds had changed. (It was me who told her her taste buds would change. I don't know if it's true, but it's what Slimey said to Mum, so I hope it is.)

We have agreed and made a solemn pact that in the spring we shall become veggies. I, of course, could become one immediately, since we won't be having roast turkey anytime soon, but it seems better to keep the Skinbag company and start at the same time so that we can encourage each other when our spirits flag or our carnivore appetites threaten to get the better of us. Also I don't want Mum gloating. I'll tell her the good news after Christmas and not before.

Tonight it's Halloween, and some kids are roaming the streets dressed up as ghouls and ghosts and skeletons. Slimey said, "Don't you go trick-or-treating?" But it's something I have never done. I don't know why; I just haven't. Skinny doesn't either. Slimey said that next year we must make it a "Big Thing" and have some fun. He likes to make Big Things of things. On Saturday it's Guy Fawkes night, and he's taking me and Mum and Skin to a fireworks display. I'm looking forward to it, believe it or not.

Tuesday

I'm reading Slimey's book. It's called *I Capture the Castle* by a person with a very strange name— Dodie Smith. What kind of name is Dodie? A strange one! But the book is great. Very funny and yet romantic!

It's all about a girl named Cassandra who wants to be a writer and is keeping a diary, just like I am, except that she lives in a ruined castle and her family doesn't have very much money; in fact, they don't have any money at all because her father, who is also a writer, sits up in the turret and reads books all day. It's so cold that Cassandra has to sit on the drain board wrapped up in a blanket with her feet in the sink to write in her diary. She has a beautiful older sister named Rose and an odd but equally beautiful stepmother named Topaz, who used to be an artist's model. The romance comes when two Americans, Neil and Simon, arrive on the scene. Simon is old and has a beard, but Neil is gorgeous. This is as far as I've gotten. I think that Rose will marry Simon and that Cassandra, maybe, will fall in love with Neil.

Oh, I nearly forgot. There is also a cute but rather dopey boy named Steven. Steven loves Cassandra and Cassandra is very fond of him but not in the way that he would like. The family owe Steven a great deal because he works for them for nothing and also goes out and earns money, which he gives to them. Without him, they wouldn't survive.

I have never read a book quite like this before; I can't wait to get back to it! I thought after horror stories, it would be slow and boring, but it's not at all. Skinny is going to read it when I've finished.

Thursday

I forgot to write yesterday.

Friday

Stewed sewage and sludge. Thank goodness we have decided to be veggies!

Saturday

This morning we went to buy some fish for the pond. Fish, I think, are basically uninteresting. All they do is swim up and down and gobble with their mouths.

I kept pointing out pretty fish I thought we should buy, but these, it seems, were warm-water fish and not suited to outdoor life. They wouldn't be, would they? Mum said, "Oh, for goodness' sake, Cherry, stop being so picky! You know perfectly well this is a pond, not an aquarium." I said, "If we had an aquarium, we could have some of the pretty ones." At least you could sit and enjoy them that way. Mum snapped (she is always snapping these days), "If it weren't for Roly, you wouldn't have anything!"

I beg her pardon. If it weren't for Roly, I could have my dog.

Now the pond is full of boring old fish that you can't even see half the time. If we had a dog, he could jump in and chase them.

I nearly forgot to mention that this evening we all went to the fireworks display. It was up in the park. Skinny doesn't like the loud ones, but I do! The louder, the better is what I say. (Mum and Slimey like the colorful ones. Wouldn't you know it?)

me   Roly   Mum

Sunday

Oh, ho-ho! Something has eaten the fish. They think it might be a heron. I'm sorry for the fish but herons need to eat and if silly human beings go digging ponds in their backyards and filling them with food, what do they expect? They might just as well write a big sign saying:

Mum says I am cruel and heartless, but I'm not. It's in a heron's nature to eat fish. They're programmed to eat fish. They can't do anything else. It's what the fish expect. And anyway Mum still eats shrimp; she says it's her "one weakness." What are shrimp, if not fish? I told her this, and she snapped (again), "That is not the point!"

So if that is not the point, what is?

Dear Carol,

I am too mad to be civil. I am almost too mad to write. Cherry is trying my patience beyond the limits!

Yesterday we stocked the pond with fish, and this morning, when we woke up, almost all of them were gone (a heron, we think). Roly was devastated. He had already begun to name them. There was Goldilocks and the Cheeky Chappie and Bright Eyes. Bright Eyes is still with us, but Goldilocks and the Cheeky Chappie are both gone. Two of his favorites! Cherry thought it was funny. She actually laughed. She made some joke about putting up a sign saying Breakfast This Way. Then she said, quite rudely, that I still ate shrimp, so what was I so upset about?

I tell you, I could have slapped her. She simply tramples over all of Roly's emotions. She is too young to realize what a rare and precious thing it is to find a man who has feelings and isn't afraid of showing them. I suppose she takes it as some kind of weakness, and like a typical bully, she can't resist putting the boot in.

Roly, as usual, speaks up in her defense. He says that

you can't really bond with a fish and that she is quite right; herons have to eat. She could still try to be a little sympathetic! Roly has slaved over that pond in an attempt to please her. How far do you have to go to try to keep your children happy?

To the ends of the earth, says Roly, if that is what it takes. We bring them into this world, he says; they do not ask to be born. I replied that he played no part in bringing this particular little terror into the world, but he says that he has crashed her living space and hijacked her mother and that she has every right to show her displeasure.

I don't think she has!

Lots of love,

Patsy

P.S. Forgive self-pity and bad manners; I know I'm a rotten correspondent. But Cherry is so trying!

P.P.S. Don't forget, I want a photograph!

Monday

I wish I hadn't laughed about his stupid fish. He spent ages picking them out, choosing ones with personalities. Well, he said they had personalities. Maybe he really thinks they do. It's true he wouldn't have had time to get attached to them, I don't think, but I can see that it was a bit upsetting for him. He is soft when it comes to animals, and as a matter of fact, so am I, which is why I'm glad I've decided after Christmas to give up eating them. Mum is giving them up because of Slimey, but I'm giving them up on principle. Also because I don't want to be poisoned, but that's really only a small part of it.

I'm not sure why Skinny is doing it. Maybe just because of me. She does like animals, but I don't think she truly appreciates how lucky she is to have a dog. Sometimes she grumbles about having to take Lulu for her walks. I would never do that. If I had a dog I would take it out happily every single day.

my dream

I thought of telling Slimey that I was sorry I laughed at his fish, but if I did, Mum would think it was only because she got mad at me and Slimey would definitely tell her. They tell each other everything. When I'm married I'll still want to have secrets. *If* I get married. (It might be difficult, living in a cardboard box.)

Tuesday

Found out about Parents' Evening and called Dad. He said, "Right! Got it. It's going in my date book. Have you told your mother?" So I went and told Mum and she wailed, "Oh, Cherry! Did you have to?" I said, "Have to what?" and she said, "Invite your father!" I said, "It's *Parents' Evening.*" And Dad is my parent.

There wasn't very much that she could say to that.

I know why she doesn't want him there. It's because she wants to drag Slimey along with us. Well, it's *my* school, and Dad's *my* parent, and he's going to come whether Mum likes it or not!

Wednesday

Told Skinny about Dad coming to Parents' Evening. She said, "What about Roly?" I said, "What about him? He's not my dad!" Skinny said she knew that, but wouldn't he be hurt?

Why should he be hurt? Someday he can go to Bernard Butter's rotten Parents' Evening.

Friday

Forgot to write yesterday. I keep forgetting to write. I forgot last week, as well, only then it was Wednesday. And all I wrote on Thursday was one line. Partly this is because of the gigantic amount of homework they give us at school and partly because I have to stay late for rehearsals and partly because I want to get back to my book. The *I Capture the Castle* book. I'm nearly at the end of it and am getting worried about what's going to happen. I couldn't bear it if Rose got Neil.

Saturday

She did! She got him! And Cassandra ended up with boring old Simon. If it hadn't been for that, it would have been one of the very best books I've ever read. Well, it still is one of the best books I have read but I think Dodie Smith got the ending wrong. I'm going to write a note to Slimey and tell him so. And then I'm going to put the note under the door of the back room where he does his elves.

I have written the note. It's a nice one to make up for laughing about his fish.

This is what I wrote:

Dear Roly,
I read I Capture the Castle by Dodie Smith and I think if she had gotten the ending right it would have been an extremely good book. Unfortunately she got it wrong by letting Rose go off with Neil and leaving Cassandra with Simon who is too old and boring and has a beard. Apart from that, I thought it was a very interesting book, which I enjoyed reading. Now I am going to lend it to my friend the Melon and see what she thinks. But I think she will agree with me about Simon.
xxx Cherry

I put in the xxx bit just to be polite.

Sunday

Sereena came over for tea. It was Mum's idea. I kept waiting eagerly for her to start telling some kind of dirty jokes, but she just sat there looking like she's made of marshmallow, all sweet and gooey.

Marshmallow Sereena

Double YUCK!

It was repulsive! Especially because I happen to know what she's really like. I told her about Slimey's book, and she said it sounded as though it would be too grown-up for her. How two-faced can you get? She said, "I'm still reading Judy Blume." "Oh, you mean like *Forever*?" I said, kicking at her ankle underneath the table. Her satellite dishes went huge as flying saucers. She said, "That's a racy one, isn't it? My mum wouldn't like it if I read that."

Mum said, "Three cheers for your mum!" which was a totally meaningless remark, considering she hasn't the faintest idea what *Forever* is about. At least,

I don't think she has. It was also hypocritical, since she's never stopped me from reading what I've wanted. She was just sucking up to Sereena.

I was really disappointed in this girl. Talk about acting! Now of course Mum is convinced she's the kindest thing there ever was and is trying to talk Mrs. Swaddle into sending her to Ruskin Manor next term. She thinks she would be a good influence on me. Ha!

Dear Carol,

Things go from bad to worse. Now she won't even talk to Roly but simply puts notes under his door! Well, one note. She says she liked I Capture the Castle but thought the ending was wrong. She thought Cassandra should have fallen for Neil, since Simon is too old and has a beard. I pointed out rather tartly that if she had read the book properly, she would have noticed that he shaved it off, but she said she had read it properly and she knows he shaved it off but it didn't make any difference; she still thought of him as having a beard. She said that he was "a beardy sort of person" and that Rose falling for Neil ruined the entire story.

Roly says she is simply exercising her critical skills. He also says that her note shows she is willing at last to start a dialogue. Some dialogue!

The little girl up the street came to tea this afternoon. Sereena. I personally find her delightful—quite refreshingly innocent—and would be happy if she and Cherry became friends, but Cherry is being her usual churlish self. Whenever I mention Sereena's name, she either chuckles, as if I've said something amusing, or she rolls her eyes and groans, as if I've said something incredibly moronic. Roly, surprisingly enough, has not taken to her. Sereena, I mean. He said there is something that doesn't quite ring true, but he can't put his finger on it. I told him that he has lived with my daughter for too long and has forgotten what nice children are like!

Who'd be a mother? Tell your gorgeous Hunk that you intend to preserve your sanity and remain childless!

All my love,

Patsy

Monday

When I got home from school today, there was a package waiting for me from America! I tore it open and inside was a box with a picture of an armadillo on it and a label that said Armadillo Droppings. An armadillo looks like this:

Armadillo droppings look like this:

They're round and squishy and you can eat them! Of course they are just toffees. Mum said, "Trust Texans!" and shuddered when I offered her one. She said, "They'll stick to your teeth." Slimey, on the other hand, ate two and said they were "yummy" (which is the sort of word that he likes to use). For once I have to agree with him. They are incredibly, scrumptiously yummy! I ate four, one after another, until Mum told me to stop being piglike, which is unfair to pigs who are actually not greedy animals, left to themselves. Anyway, I thought I had better stop before I'd eaten them all. I want to take them to school tomorrow and see people's faces when I say, "Have an armadillo turd!"

Now I suppose I must write and say thank you. It's much easier to pick up the telephone and call Texas, but Mum would have a fit, so I'd better not.

Tuesday

I took the armadillo droppings to school, and everyone thought it was hilarious except for Mrs.

James, who said, "What on earth have you got there, Cherry?" and when I showed her she made a face and said, "That's what I call poor taste." I don't call it poor taste! I call it delicious! She should have tried one, but she wouldn't. Some people have no sense of humor.

I went over to Sereena's house when I got home from school and showed her the box (which was now empty). I waited till we were in her bedroom because I didn't think her mother would like it. All Sereena said was "I bet they didn't look anything like the real thing!" I said, "They did. They looked just like it." She said, "How do you know? Have you ever seen an armadillo dropping?" I had to admit that I hadn't. Then she told me something really gross.

She said that her best friend's brother works as a cameraman for a TV crew, and one day they went into this prison to make a film, and they wanted to show the prisoners emptying their toilet buckets. She said, "They didn't want to use the real thing 'cause that would be too smelly, so they made up a yellow mixture with lemonade powder, and then they got some brown Play-Doh and rolled it in oats and dropped it into the lemonade water with bits of toilet paper, and you couldn't tell the difference." She said, "That's the sort of thing they do when they make films."

Ugh! I think that's far nastier than armadillo droppings. And that was in *England*.

Wednesday

When I got home from school, Mum told me that there had been a telephone call from Dad, saying that unfortunately he wouldn't be able to get to Parents' Evening after all because he had a meeting to attend and wouldn't be finished in time. Mum said, "I'm sorry, sweetheart. I know you really wanted him to come."

It isn't very often that Mum calls me things like *sweetheart*. I knew it was because she was feeling sorry for me, and not wanting to gloat (even though she'd said all along that Dad wouldn't show up).

"It's quite a long way for him to travel," she said, trying, I suppose, to make things seem better.

I said, "He promised!" But what do grown-ups' promises mean?

I tried calling Skinny Melon, thinking it would be nice to have a laugh about something—anything, really—but all Melon wanted to do was moan about our math homework, which she said she didn't understand. If the Melon can't understand it, I certainly won't be able to. I'm not going to bother with it. Why should I?

Thursday

Tomorrow is Parents' Evening, which a few days ago I was looking forward to. Now I just think it's a drag. Last year Mum went on her own. This year she's making me go with her. She's also taking Slime, which is what she wanted all along.

I said, "Why do I have to come?" She said, "Because you're the one it's all about." So then I said, "Why does he have to come?" and she said, "If you're referring to Roly, it's because he's just as interested in your welfare as I am." Then she added, "Though sometimes I wonder why he bothers."

I haven't asked him to bother. I don't want him to come. Trying to get around me, Mum said, "Surely it will be nicer for you to have both of us there?" I said, "Why?" And she said, "Well, it's normal to have two parents, isn't it?" I said, "Not really. Not these days. There's lots of kids with only one." To which she snapped, "So what have you been making all the fuss about?"

What fuss? I never made any fuss.

She said, "If there are all these other kids whose parents have divorced, what's so special about you?"

I never said there was anything special. And just because I'm not the only one whose mum and dad have split up doesn't make it any better. It's my dad I care about.

I didn't say any of this to Mum. We don't ever really talk about things like that. We just get mad at each other, and she snaps and tells me I'm selfish and ungracious, which is what she did now.

It's true I was in a bad mood tonight. I don't know why. Sometimes I just am.

friday

As we were about to leave for school for Parents' Evening, Slimey suddenly said, "Cherry, do you mind me coming along? I won't, if you'd rather I didn't."

It made me feel terrible. He'd got dressed up in his best clothes. He looks all funny and peculiar in them, like a sort of long floppy beanstalk inside a suit. His pants bag at the back because he hasn't got any butt, and his pockets sag because he keeps things in them. Pens and pencils and little notebooks for drawing. I wanted to say that as far as I was concerned, I'd rather he didn't come, but I couldn't bring myself to do that. I just mumbled something like "That's all right, I don't mind." His face went into this big happy beam, and that was that. I was stuck with him. It wouldn't have been bad if they hadn't looked so odd, what with Mum being fat with the baby and Slimey being all beanstalky and thin, they made a weird couple.

We were the *only people* who didn't drive up in a car. At least, I should think we were. Amanda Miles said to me the other day, "Can't your dad afford a car?" I don't know how she knew he didn't have one, but anyway, I pointed out that he's not my dad.

And as I also pointed out, he could probably afford half a dozen cars if he wanted them. With the number of elves he draws, he ought to be able to. I said, "It's a matter of principle. He happens to care about this earth and the creatures that live on it." She said, "What are you talking about?" I said, "Pollution. Cars ought to be done away with," and she said, "Oh, that's ridiculous!"

I used to think it was, but now I'm not so sure. Slimey pointed out the other day that all the fir trees up and down our street have gone brown and died. All of them. Mum says maybe it's a tree disease, but Slimey and I think it's acid rain.

Parents' Evening was quite embarrassing, actually. I knew it would be. I had to stand there while Mum and Slimey talked to all the teachers. I could just feel people like Amanda Miles looking at Slimey and snickering. And then old Slimey keeps making these dumb jokes, and some of the teachers are polite and pretend it's funny while some of them—Miss Milsom, for instance, she's really sour—just pinch their lips together and make their nostrils flare, and you can tell they're thinking, "What an idiot!"

As a matter of fact, I felt a bit sorry for him. I mean, he's completely ludicrous-looking, with his scraggly beard and this huge Adam's apple that keeps bobbing up and down every time he swallows and these enormous hands and feet that go clump, clump, clump everywhere. He's really clumsy too. But he does try hard to be liked, and I guess it's not his fault he keeps doing it wrong. He just doesn't know any better. I didn't like the thought of Amanda laughing at him. I wanted to tell her that at least old Slimey doesn't go around eating animals or poisoning the planet with noxious fumes like I bet her dad does. Drawing elves might strike some people as a pretty drippy thing to do, but no one can deny that it's harmless. And I suppose if you were only four years old, it might bring pleasure to your little babyish life. I expect I probably even liked elves when I was four years old.

Actually I'm not being fair to Slimey. He doesn't just draw elves. He doesn't really draw elves at all. Just in this one particular book that he did. Mostly he draws animals and people. Funny animals and people. Even his elves were funny elves.

I wish I could draw like he can.

↑ my elves

Saturday

Sereena wanted to know whether I would go and have tea with her again, but I said I couldn't because I was going swimming with Skinny Melon. Mum got upset when she heard. She said, "Why couldn't Sereena go with you?" It's hard to explain that Skinny and I don't want anyone with us. We're a pair. We like being alone together. Mum ought to understand, since she seems to like being on her own with Slimey.

I told this to Skinny, and she said that Mum probably likes being with Slimey because he makes her laugh. She said, "He's really funny, he ought to be on TV."

Slimey?

Dad called tonight. He said he was very sorry he hadn't been able to come to Parents' Evening. "But you know how it is . . . meetings that go on forever." I said that it was all right. I added that he hadn't really missed much. He said, "No, but I do feel bad about it."

I was going to suggest that maybe he could come to the school play instead and hear me sing, but before I could do so he was called away by Rosemary. I could hear her voice yelling at him. "Greg, are you coming?" Dad said, "Oops, got to go! I'll call you back tomorrow."

I've decided that I hate Rosemary.

Sunday

Wonders will never cease! Slimey has shaved off his beard!!! Unfortunately he looks even more peculiar without it. He has these rabbit teeth and hardly any chin.

Spot the difference:

What does Mum see in him?

I know what she sees in him. It's what Skinny says; Mum thinks he's funny. And he doesn't shout or lose his temper. I've never heard him shout. He has a quiet sort of voice. And he does these silly nice things, like the other day, for instance, when we were walking up the street and he saw this worm in the middle of the pavement. Instantly he stopped and broke a bit of twig off someone's hedge so that he could pick it up and put it in the grass. He said it would dry out if it were left where it was.

There aren't many people who would care about a worm. I wouldn't have done that before. Dad used to go into the garden and tread on snails. Not on purpose but because they happened to be in his way. Slimey would never do that. He steps over them. Whenever I go into the garden early in the morning, he says, "Watch out for snails!" It used to madden me, but I've gotten used to it. I suppose you can learn to live with most things.

The only thing I will never accept is Mum breaking her promise about my dog. How could she do that to me?

141 Arethusa Road
London W5
20 November

My dear Carol,

So very many thanks for the armadillo droppings (a great success with my crude daughter!) and for the mug shot of your DHT (Divinely Handsome Texan!). What is he doing working for a bank??? Why isn't he in the movies? On second thought, keep him at the bank! He's safer there.

I must tell you that Roly has shaved off his beard. I feel a bit guilty about it. He grew that beard when he was twenty to cover up the fact that he doesn't have much of a chin. Poor love! Now I honestly think he looks far better with a beard. But Cherry hated it—not that she actually said so, but she has ways of making her feelings obvious—and as you know, he will go to almost any lengths in his efforts to please her.

This all came about, the beard thing, because on Friday it was Parents' Night at Cherry's school, and Roly was happy to come along and "be a normal parent," as he put it, but he was scared that Cherry might not want him to. He asked her if she minded, and surprisingly she was polite and said no, which delighted Roly. But later

160

that evening, after she was in bed, he suddenly said, "She was ashamed of me, wasn't she?" Of course I indignantly said no—what right has Cherry to be ashamed of Roly?—but nothing would shift his conviction.

He jumped up and went over to the mirror and said, "Look at me! I'm just a mess! If I want her to be proud of having me for a father, I'm going to have to get my act together."

So now he has shaved off his beard and, Carol, it's such a mistake! With the beard he looks like what he is—an artist. Now he looks like a—a chinless wonder! Only I haven't the heart to tell him. He is absolutely convinced that Cherry will prefer him like this. I don't think I could bear it if she made some hurtful comment. It's truly frightening, the power that children have.

Remember! Stick to your guns with the DHT . . . you are a career woman!

All my love,

Patsy

Monday

Amanda Miles asked me today, "Was that your stepfather with you on Friday?" I couldn't think who she was talking about at first, since I don't think of Slimey as being my stepfather, but I suppose he is. So I said, "Yes. Why?" And she gave this silly smirk and said, "Oh, I just wondered." I felt like pinching her.

Tuesday

Nothing very much happened today.

Wednesday

Nor today.

Thursday

Nothing seems to be happening at all in my life right now.

Friday

Dad never called me last Sunday, like he promised. Maybe he will this Sunday. If that woman lets him.

Skinny came home with me after school, and we watched a video, but she couldn't stay the night, since she has to visit her gran over the weekend. She said, "Weird Melvin's going to drive us there in his fancy car." I said, "What's he got? A Mercedes?" Skinny didn't know. "Something big and shiny," is all she could come up with. She's useless with things like that.

"I think we ought to go by train," she said. "Otherwise we're polluting the atmosphere."

She picked that up from Slimey. She'd never have thought of it herself.

Saturday

I don't know how much longer I can go on writing in this diary. It's very difficult when life is completely empty. I know it's good practice if I want to be a writer one day, but if books are still around when I grow up, I think I would rather draw the pictures that go inside them than have to write the words. I am actually quite good at drawing. This, for instance, is Slimey before and after:

Sunday

It rained all day. Dad still didn't call.

Dear Carol,

I just got your letter in which you remind me that when we were young and read I Capture the Castle, we held exactly the same view as Cherry regarding men with beards.

You say, "I couldn't bear the thought of Cassandra being stuck with Simon. To an eleven-year-old he seemed practically senile!" Yes, you're quite right. One forgets, perhaps, what it's like to be eleven years old.

And I have been thinking, too, about what I wrote last week. That bit where I said what power children wield. They don't, of course, compared with adults. We're the ones who decide their lives for them—what they're going to be called, where they're going to school, where they're going to live—who they're going to live with. It wasn't Cherry's decision that Greg and I split up. The only power she's exercising is the power to strike back. I just wish she wouldn't pick on Roly. But children instinctively go for the weakest spot. She knows very well that by hurting Roly she hurts me.

I'm feeling a bit down at the moment. Beginning to

doubt if things will ever be right. Cherry is obviously never going to forgive me for splitting with Greg, and that means she is never going to accept Roly. What a mess!

But life at least is beginning to work for you. You've been through the dark days and come through them. And I don't ever remember you moaning and groaning the way I do.

All love from your wimpish,

Patsy

Monday

Asked the Melon if she'd found out what car Weird Melvin drives, and she said she'd forgotten to look. She said she's not interested in his car. She's not interested in him. She wishes her mum had never met him. She is sick and tired of him always being there.

I said I knew how she felt because it was exactly what I'd felt when Mum started going out with Slimey Roland. I thought this was the sort of thing she would like to hear, but all she did was snap at me. She said, "That was totally different!"

How? That is what I'd like to know. The Melon is becoming very grumpy these days.

No card from Slimey in a while. Perhaps he got the message at last?

Tuesday

I hope Mum hasn't gone and told old Slime that I throw his cards in the wastebasket. It's just the mean sort of thing she'd do. I think I'll go and take them out and put them where she can't find them.

I've taken them out. I've put them in a box under the bed. Now I suppose she'll think I've stopped striking and am going to start tidying the rest of my room.

If that's what she thinks, then she's wrong. I have only done it so that I won't hurt Slime's feelings.

Wednesday

Dad called. He said he's been very "tied up" at the office. He also said that he hasn't forgotten his promise to buy me a computer for Christmas. I expect once I get used to it, I'll find it interesting. At the moment I'm more into drawing and painting. A big package of books arrived for Slimey today. They were all the same book, from the publisher. One of his Freddy the Frog books. Freddy the Frog looks like this:

not a very good
picture of a frog →

Well, something like that. I can't quite draw it as well as Slimey does, but he's had lots more practice than me. I bet I could if I kept at it.

← better frogs

I meant to ask Dad about coming to see me in the school play, but I forgot. I don't expect it matters. I don't expect he'd have been able to come. He'd probably have a meeting or be headed out to a dinner party. I understand that it's difficult for him, being so busy and living so far away. Also I don't expect Rosemary would have let him come.

Thursday

Twenty-four days until Christmas! I wonder what Mum will buy me?

Friday

I asked Slimey Roland at teatime whether he was a crusty roll and butter or a soft roll and butter. I thought that was a good joke. So did Roly. He laughed. Mum didn't. I don't think Mum has much of a sense of humor. She never appreciates my jokes. She said, "He's a great big softie, as you well know, and you'd do anything to take advantage of that!"

She's always accusing me of these things. I don't know what she means.

I've been drawing frogs all day long and can now make them almost as good as Slimey's.

Saturday

He pushed another card under my door last night. He's not so bad really, I suppose. It's just that he's not my dad!

Sunday

Today I took out all Slimey's cards and read them, which I never really bothered to do before. Once you get used to it, it's easy. At first you have to think a bit, but then you learn the symbols, like he always draws a 🐝 for words like *he* or *we*. And a 🪢

for *not*. I'm going to write out what they say and practice doing it myself. It would be fun to write picture messages in Christmas cards.

Dear Cherry,
I'm sorry that cats and dogs make me sneeze. What about a turtle?
    Love, Roly

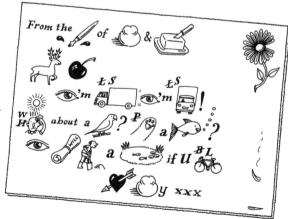

Dear Cherry,
I'm sorry,* I'm sorry! What about a bird? Or a fish? I will dig a pond if you like.
    Love, Roly

Lorry is the British word for "truck."

Dear Cherry,
We can have goldfish,
snails, bullrushes,*
and water lilies. It
will be fun!
   Love, Roly

*Bullrush is the British
word for "cattail."

Dear Cherry,
Please don't eat us!
   Love, Roly

Dear Cherry,
Well done! You will
make an excellent
angel!
   Love, Roly

Dear Cherry,
Here are four examples
of egg jokes. Exercising,
expelled, exit, exacting.
Silly, aren't they?
  Love, Roly

Dear Cherry,
If Sunday is nice
maybe we'll go for
a picnic.*
  Love, Roly

*Knickers is the
British word for
"underpants."

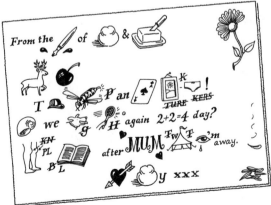

Dear Cherry,
That was an ace
picnic! Shall we do
it again someday?
Please look after
Mum when I'm
away.
  Love, Roly

Dear Cherry,
It's ace to be back! I miss you and Mum when I'm not here. PS, Here is something for you. I hope you like her!
    Love, Roly

Dear Cherry,
Did you like Snow White? I did! Can you say who all these are?
    Love, Roly

Dear Cherry,
I hope you are happy about the baby. I'm very happy! I think a baby will be fun!
    Love, Roly

Dear Cherry,
Have you read a book
called I Capture the
Castle? It's good. Take
it with you to read on
holiday.*
    Love, Roly

*Holiday is the British
word used to refer to
a vacation or trip.

Dear Cherry,
Welcome home! Good
to have you back. We
miss you when you are
not here.
    Love, Roly

Dear Cherry,
It's good to have a
pond. Foxes, badgers,
and hedgehogs can
drink there and it
might bring frogs
and toads.
    Love, Roly

175

Dear Cherry,
I'm happy that you
like the book but sad
you didn't like poor
Simon and his beard.
Maybe he looked okay
when he shaved it off?
Love, Roly

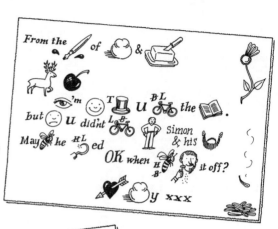

Dear Cherry,
I hope you like me
better now that I
have no beard!
Love, Roly

Dear Cherry,
I'm crusty when I'm
cross and soft when I'm
not cross. Today I'm not
cross, I'm happy!* It will
soon be Christmas!
Love, Roly

*Nappy is the British word
for "diaper."

176

I just realized what the little symbols are down the sides of the notes.

He always does these little pic‐ tures of a flower. She loves me, she loves me not . . .

There aren't many petals left now. I wonder what he'll do when he gets to the end?

I'm not sure that I like him, but he's definitely not as bad as I used to think.

Monday

Tuesday

Today we had cow dung and cardboard patties for lunch. Well, that's what I had. Skinny Melon had what looked like armadillo droppings in greasy dishwater. We both had stomachaches, dizziness, and a feeling of total norseea. Norsea?

I haven't been recording school meals lately. This is not because they've been good but simply because I have had too many other things to think about. Like the play! Old Roly the Rat and Mum are both going to come, though Mum is thinking of bringing earplugs in case my loud untuneful voice frightens the baby, which she says it could, even though it is still in the woom. I told her my singing will give it a feeling for music, but Mum only laughed. Mum is very rude about my singing. All I can say is, she is in for a Big Surprise!

One of the girls in the play, Davina Walters, stayed for an angel rehearsal the other day. When I had finished my solo, she cried, "That's it, Cherry baby! Sock it to 'em!" And Miss Burgess told Amanda, who is another angel, that she ought to "take a leaf out of Cherry's book." She said, "Her voice may not always be in tune but at least it can be heard."

She only said it wasn't in tune because she didn't want to make Amanda jealous. Amanda has a voice like a sick cow.

I've given up the idea of asking Dad to come. If he said yes and then at the last minute found he was too busy, I'd be disappointed and hurt so I think it's best not to raise false hopes.

Wednesday

I looked those words up. It's *nausea* and *womb*. Why is *womb* pronounced "woom" and *comb* pronounced "coam"?

I sent a picture message to Skinny Melon in class today, and now we're going to do it all the time but not with Mrs. James or Miss Milsom because they could be mean if we got caught.

Thursday

Green tadpoles in schmelt sauce. Yeeeurgh!

Friday

Horse-dropping tarts. I just don't believe they could have been mushrooms. They were brown. Whoever heard of brown mushrooms?

Dad just phoned! He said, "I haven't got anything special to talk about but I thought I'd call and say hello and find out how you're doing." I said I was doing well except for math and computers and also home ec, where Mrs. Marshall despairs of me. I know this for a fact because she said so. She said, "Cherry Waterton, I despair of you." This was because I sewed a hem all wrong and she had to unpick it and start again, and when she gave it back to me, I said, "I'm left-handed, does it matter?" And of course it did because I sew from a different direction.

I told this to Dad, and he laughed and said, "All the best people are left-handed." I wonder if this is true. I just realized that old Ratty is, though I didn't say this to Dad.

So anyway we talked for a while, and then Dad said he had to go but that we must "see each other again very soon," so before I could stop myself I said why didn't he come to the school play and hear me sing, but he said he couldn't, unfortunately, do that because he is so busy. All these Americans keep coming over, and Dad is the only person who can deal with them.

At least it's better to know now than to think he is coming and then he doesn't.

Saturday

Went shopping with Mum and Roly Rat, and I saw brown mushrooms! I never noticed them before. But the ones they dished up at school were all soft and squishy, so I still think they were horse droppings. I expect they get them cheap by the bucketful.

Sunday

Sereena came over, and I taught her how to draw picture messages. That girl has a mind like a sewer. All she could do was giggle and draw pictures of toilets and butts.

But Roly is a real artist. Sereena is just stupid. She has a one-track mind. She said something that annoyed me so much, I yelled at her. I was showing her some of Roly's picture messages, and she said that she thought they were childish. I snapped, "Oh, do you? Well, for your information that's just where you're wrong. My stepdad happens to be a famous picture book artist who has had books published in every country in the world. Even in Russia. Even in Japan."

That shut her up.

Monday

I told the Skinbag about Sereena, and Skin said that she sounded obnoxious. I said that she is and I hoped now I had snubbed her so that she would stay away from me. She had some nerve saying that about old Roly Rat's drawings. The Melon agrees. She thinks Roly is the cat's whiskers. She said today that she wished her mum could meet someone like him.

Tuesday

Only twelve days till Christmas! Mum asked me this evening what I wanted for my Christmas present and I said, "You know what I want! I want a dog."

She sighed and said, "Oh, Cherry, we've discussed this before! Roly can't help being allergic. Don't be so selfish all the time."

I don't think it's selfish to want someone to keep their promise. I said, "If I can't have what I want, then I don't want anything," which Mum said was cutting off my nose to spite my face. Whatever that's supposed to mean.

nose →

I think what it means is that I'm not going to get a dog, so I might as well accept it and find something else. But I can't think of anything else. Not anything big. I told Mum this and she said that I must be a very contented person to have so few wants. I would be contented, if I could have my dog. I would even be contented living with Slime.

Wednesday

Eleven days! I am marking them off on the calendar. It's a pity the baby is going to miss Christmas.

February seems a long time away.

Thursday

Ten days!

We had the dress rehearsal for the play this afternoon, which meant we were spared homework. Hooray! I hate Thursday afternoons, since it's math, and Mr. Fisher says I'm the only person he knows who can take one away from two and make it three. I said that was because I am a naturally creative person, and he told me not to get wise with him, but his eyes sort of crinkled as he said it, so I don't think he'll report me.

The dress rehearsal went really well. At least, it did for me. Amanda Miles and some of the others forgot their words and had to be prompted, but I was word perfect. A few of the teachers came and sat at the back of the hall and watched. At the end, one of them I don't know said, "I like the angels." Miss Burgess said, "Could you hear them all right?" And he said, "All except the little redhead" (meaning Amanda), and then he pointed at me and said, "The police could use that one as a siren." Miss Burgess said, "Oh, yes, we never have any problems with Cherry." Amanda hated me for it, you could tell.

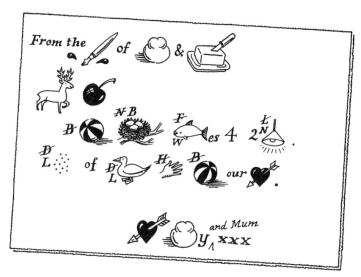

Friday

Last night old Roly Rat pushed another card under my door. It was a nice one; he made it look sort of like a telegram, so I took it to school with me and stuck it on the wall near my classroom. Everyone wanted to know what it said, so I translated it for them, and they all thought it was great, except for Amanda, who said she'd rather have a real telegram, but nobody agreed with her.

Miss Burgess told me that I ought to keep it because it might be valuable one day. She said, "It's an original drawing, and your stepfather is famous."

Is he? I never thought of Roly Rat as *really* being famous. I didn't tell Miss Burgess I had a whole stack of his drawings at home. But I'm glad now that I didn't throw them out, which is what would have happened if I hadn't gone on strike. Mum would have simply emptied my wastebasket into the garbage. I like Ratty's cards, and I'm going to keep them to show my own kids, if I ever have any. Not because they might be valuable but because they're funny and interesting.

My performance tonight was pretty good, I think. At the end, all the angels had to bow in front of the curtain. Afterward I was driven home by Skinny Melon's mum and her boyfriend, Weird Melvin, in his car (which is a fancy, schmancy BMW!). Mum and Ratty are not coming until tomorrow night. Weird Melvin said, "Well, at least we had no trouble hearing you." And Skin's mum told me that I was a very confident performer. Skinny giggled and said, "She was the Foghorn Angel!" but I don't mind Skinny giggling, since she meant no harm.

I didn't want Mum and Roly Rat coming to the first night in case I had stage fright, but they'll be there tomorrow. I think they're looking forward to it.

Saturday

I was even better tonight! I felt like I really got into it. I'm thinking again about maybe becoming a rock star. I know I have the voice for it because that's what everyone says. A minister came up to me afterward and said, "Aha! The Angel of the Clarion Call!" Even Mum was impressed, I could tell. And a man from the local paper came to take our picture and he said, "Where's the little one with the big voice?" (Meaning me.) "Let's have her in the middle." Amanda was mad as could be!

Instead of waiting for the bus, we all went home by cab because Roly said, "It's the only way for a star to travel." Mum said, "Well! I suppose we'll have to pay to speak to you now."

This is us being photographed.

Monday

Skinny came to school this morning looking miserable. I asked her what was the matter, and she said, "Nothing." So then I said, "What did you do on Sunday?" and she said, "Nothing." I said, "I didn't do anything, either. We could have gotten together if I'd known. But I thought you were going out with Weird Melvin." She said, "We did." I said, "So how can you say that you did nothing? You must have done *something*. Even if you just drove somewhere, that's doing something. You can't call driving somewhere not doing anything. Unless you mean you were just sitting there in a great big heap. Maybe that's what you mean?"

Skin was in a strange mood. She told me in decidedly huffish tones to just shut up and stop getting on her nerves. Then she didn't speak to me again until after lunch.

Kind of odd. She's all right now, though.

Tuesday

Hooray! Mrs. James said our report cards will arrive after Christmas. I'm not sure whether this is a good thing or a bad thing. Skinny says it's bad because they'll be hanging over us, but on the other hand it avoids any bad news before the holiday. I expect my grades will be poor. Skinny expects hers will be poor too, though I don't know why, since Skinny is very quiet and well behaved. I'm the one who's always getting in trouble.

Tomorrow we're going to go buy our presents for each other and for other people. We have a rule that we won't spend more than two pounds on each other. I think this is a good rule because it stops us from feeling guilty. For instance, if I only bought Skinny a calendar with pictures of dogs (which is what I'm going to do) and she bought me a new pair of Doc Martens, then I would feel lousy.

Wednesday

I have bought:

A calendar for Skinny Melon, some leggings for Mum, some aftershave from the Body Shop for Roly Rat, and a teddy bear for the baby.

It was difficult knowing what to get for Roly Rat, but in the end I thought if I got him something from the Body Shop it would show that I care about the environment and about things not being tested on animals. That should please him.

I bought the leggings for Mum because I'm tired of seeing her in those horrible overalls. It will be good for her to wear something bright and pretty when she no longer has the baby inside and is back to normal. They're orange with swirly yellow and purple patterns. She'll look great in them. After all, she has nice legs when they're not hidden in overalls.

I bought something for the baby because although I know it's not going to be here until February, I think it should have some gifts waiting. I thought that a bear would be cute. There were all different colored ones—pink ones, yellow ones, blue ones, brown ones—so in the end I got a brown one, since we don't know whether the baby is going to be a boy or a girl.

I've been wondering which I would rather have, a brother or a sister, and I think on the whole I would rather have a brother because it would be something different. I'm looking forward to it, I suppose, now that I'm used to the idea. Skinny wants to come and look at it when it's born. She says that she likes babies. I can't imagine why, since as far as I can see they don't actually do anything except eat and sleep. Well, they also mess themselves and cry a lot and sometimes scream. They also drool. All these things are pretty revolting.

Skinny says this just goes to show how little I know about them. She says that all these things may be true but that when babies are not messing or drooling or nursing, they are sweet and cuddly and what she calls "fun." She says that it's exciting when they smile for the first time and say their first word. Hmm! We shall see.

Thursday

Today the Skinbag came for tea. I asked her if she would like to watch a video of Laurel and Hardy that belongs to Ratty, and she said okay, so I put it on and it was hilarious. I was getting a pain in my side from laughing so hard. All the while, the Melon just sat there glum and gloomy with a face like a wet dish-rag. She started to annoy me, so I switched the video off and asked sort of gruffly, "What's the matter with you? Where's your sense of humor?" Suddenly, she burst into tears and told me that life as she has known it is over.

I was completely taken aback because Skinny is definitely not a watering pot (as Mum calls it). So naturally I asked her why life as she has known it is over, and then it all came pouring out, about Weird Melvin and her mum and how her mum has just announced that they are thinking of getting married.

My immediate instinct was to make a sarcastic remark on her sudden change of attitude. It's funny that when I used to carry on about old Ratty, the Skinbag could think of nothing better to say than how lucky I was and how any dad is better than no dad and how she wished that her mum would get married again. But because I am her friend, I suppressed my instinct and told her that I know just how she's feeling, since I've been through it all myself.

"It's not the same," she says. "Roly's nice. Anyone would be glad to have Roly for a dad." And then she makes these really loud sobs and says that nobody in their right mind would want Weird Melvin.

So while I'm sitting there wondering what to say next, Mum comes in to tell us that tea's ready, and of course she sees the Melon in tears and wants to know what's wrong, so I explain the situation, and Mum goes all soft and mushy (she's never like that with me) and puts an arm around the Melon's shoulders and coaxes her out into the kitchen, where Ratty is. And before I know it, the Melon's weeping all over Ratty and saying how Weird Melvin is the pits and life as she has known it is over.

After a while she finishes blubbering and blows her nose in Ratty's hanky. (I wouldn't! It's all covered in paint.) Ratty asks her what exactly is so weird about poor old Melv. I say, "There isn't anything weird. He drives a BMW and he gives her money." But the Melon smirks at me and says he's got this big fat belly and gray hairs growing out of his nostrils and hands like clammy fungus, and he treats her as if she's about six years old. She says it's all right for Matthew (that's her brother); he's hardly ever at home. And it's all right for the Blob (her sister) because she's only eight and doesn't seem to mind if she's treated like a baby.

"But I can't stand it!" wails the Melon.

And then old Ratty said something that surprised

me. He said, "The poor man's probably terrified of you. You young girls frighten the lives out of us plain middle-aged men."

"*Do* we?" I asked in shock.

"You'd better believe it!" said Roly.

The Melon hiccuped and said that she didn't see any reason why Weird Melvin should be terrified of her.

"Because he's desperate to make a good impression," said Roly. "He's desperate for you to approve of him and it makes him nervous." And then he told her to try being kind to him and to laugh at his jokes and maybe even ask his advice about something, because that would make him feel that he was wanted. He promised that if she did, it would work miracles.

I could see that the Melon was doubtful, but at least it shut her up and stopped her dripping all over the place. When her mum came to pick her up (in her old VW), I went out to the car and reminded Skin, in what I hoped were comforting tones, that when Mum first got married to Roly, I thought he was the biggest creep ever. "And now," I said, "I like him." I said that what happened was, you sort of grow used to them.

The Melon just gave me this dying-duck look and fastened her seat belt. She was making such a big production over it. I suppose she wants to be the center of attention. Pathetic, really. I didn't make anywhere near this amount of fuss.

Incidentally, I have discovered what Mum has bought me for Christmas! It's on top of the double dresser as usual. She always puts my presents up there. She thinks I don't know, but I found out years ago. It's not really cheating to look, since it's only the smaller gifts. My big gifts she hides somewhere else in a place I haven't yet discovered.

I only took a very quick peek. Some of the gifts are in bags, and when they are in bags, I don't look. That's one of my rules. But I saw a couple of CDs that I really wanted, so that's good. There are also what I think are books (flat and hard) and maybe even clothes (soft when you poke them). That's good, too!

Friday

Today I had a minor heart attack. I went with Mum to do some last-minute shopping (Roly Rat stayed behind to draw some last-minute elves). We walked through the tights and leggings department, and Mum suddenly said, "Maybe I'll buy myself a pair of leggings. What do you think?" and she headed straight for the very pair that I had bought for her! Quickly I said, "You don't want those. What about these?" pointing to a drab and boring pair. To my great relief she said, "Yes, I suppose those are more suited to a woman my age, aren't they?" It was a tense moment!

I wrapped up all my presents and put little gift tags on them with picture messages.

Roly's says...

Mum's says:

I am going to clean my room for Christmas.

Saturday

Today I felt the baby move! Mum said, "Oh! He's kicking me."

"Or, she," I said. "It might be a she." Mum agreed that it might be.

I don't mind which it is.

The Melon called in the evening to wish me a merry Christmas. She said that Weird Melvin was going to be with them for three whole days but that it was "all right" because she had done what Roly suggested and asked Weird Melvin's advice about something. She had asked what sort of plant she could grow in a dark part of the garden (old Skin is into gardening), and he had come up with some good ideas. It seems he knows a lot about plants, so now she doesn't mind so much about the fungusy hands and gray nose hairs and the big fat belly. What she actually said was "He's not as weird as I thought."

Thank goodness for that! It means I can enjoy Christmas without having to worry about Skin. She is my best friend—my *very* best friend—and I wouldn't have liked to think of her being unhappy.

My dear Carol,

I am writing this on Christmas Eve. Haven't had a chance until now, what with one thing and another.

Last Saturday we went to see Cherry sing in the school play. Oh, dear! What can I say? They obviously chose her because she looked right—very pretty and impish. But she can't sing! Of course we told her she was the greatest, or at any rate Roly did. As a result, she has been blasting our eardrums ever since. I wish she would take up something quiet, like painting.

Roly bought her a set of pens, paints, crayons, drawing pads, etc., for Christmas, but since it's from him, she'll probably just look at it with that terrible expression of condescension and contempt that eleven-year-old girls often have. Do you know what I mean? Cold and cutting and, oh, so knowing and superior! Were we ever like that when we were eleven?

In fairness to her, I have to say that she's been quite sweet and considerate these last few days (apart from the ear-blasting).

A funny thing happened the other day. I was going to

buy myself a pair of leggings, and Cherry practically tied herself in knots trying to guide me away from a particular pair she had obviously bought me for Christmas! I'll have to pretend I'm totally surprised when I open her gift, just as Cherry will pretend total surprise when she opens some of hers. Not very much is a secret in this house. She always climbs up to look on top of the double dresser because she knows that's where I keep all her "pillowcase" presents. She's been doing it for years. It's a game we sort of play, except that she doesn't know that I know she does it! (Don't worry, I've hidden your baseball bat! I tucked it away the minute it arrived.)

I'm a little worried that she hasn't bought anything for Roly. I've kept dropping hints, but the only kind of hint she understands is the kind that you apply with a sledgehammer! She is incredibly thick-skinned. So I've got some aftershave from the Body Shop and gift-wrapped it, just to be on the safe side. He would be terribly hurt if she forgot him.

Meanwhile, we have a real surprise for her! I won't tell you what it is. See if you can guess!

A few weeks ago, in the middle of the night, Roly shot bolt upright in bed and cried, "I've got it!" When I asked, "Got what?" he said, "The solution. I'm allergic to fur, not skin. We'll get her a hairless one!"

So we hunted high and low—and, incidentally, paid the earth, though Roly assures me it will be worth it for the pleasure it will bring—and all I will say is that it is HAIRLESS, that it comes originally from CHINA, and that right at this moment it is up the street being looked after by Mrs. Swaddle (the mother of Sereena).

Have you guessed?

Roly is going to go over and get it tomorrow before breakfast. I can't wait to see Cherry's face!

Greg, hard to believe, has kept his word for once and sent her the computer. It was delivered last week while she was at school. I'm sure it will be very useful, but I can tell you now that between a hairless Chinese what-not and a computer, there will be no competition!

I do hope you and your Dwayne have the most wonderful Christmas ever. If I could only rid myself of fear that (a.) Cherry will have forgotten to buy something for Roly and that (b.) she is going to resent the baby, I would be the happiest soul on earth! I will keep my fingers crossed. Maybe I am misjudging her.

All my fondest love,

Patsy

From the 🖌️ of ☁️ & 🧈

This is Charlie Chan. He is 4U. When he grows up he will look like this ↓

👁️ 🐍 U B/L 🚲 him!

RH

❤️→ ☁️ y∧ xxx and Mum xxx

She
loves
you!

Christmas Day

Dear Roly,
Charlie Chan is the best present
I've ever received. He makes me so
happy. I adore him already! Thank
you, thank you, thank you!
Love, Cherry XXX

Christmas

Now that I have my beautiful Charlie, I won't be
keeping this diary anymore. I'll be far too busy taking
him for walks! So this is where I'm going to end. It's
been fun, and I think I accomplished what Mrs.
James said I would; I cleaned out the cupboard. But
from now on, I'm going to concentrate more on
drawing than on writing. I've decided . . . when I
grow up I'm going to be an *artist*!